if I should
LOSE YOU

First published 2012 by
FREMANTLE PRESS

This edition first published 2024.

Fremantle Press Inc. trading as Fremantle Press
PO Box 158, North Fremantle, Western Australia, 6159
fremantlepress.com.au

Cover images iStock, istockphoto.com and Shutterstock, shutterstock.com
Designed by Nada Backovic, nadabackovic.com
Printed and bound by IPG

 A catalogue record for this
book is available from the
National Library of Australia

ISBN 9781760993085 (paperback)
ISBN 9781760993092 (ebook)

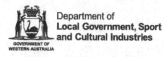

Fremantle Press is supported by the State Government through the
Department of Local Government, Sport and Cultural Industries.

Fremantle Press respectfully acknowledges the Whadjuk people of the
Noongar nation as the Traditional Owners and Custodians of the land
where we work in Walyalup.

if I should
LOSE YOU
NATASHA
LESTER

 FREMANTLE PRESS

ABOUT THE AUTHOR

Natasha Lester worked as a marketing executive for L'Oréal before turning her hand to writing. She won the Hungerford Award for her first novel *What is Left Over After*. Since then, she's become a New York Times–bestselling author of eight historical novels, including *The French Photographer*, *The Paris Secret*, *The Riviera House*, *The Three Lives of Alix St Pierre* and *The Disappearance of Astrid Bricard*. Her books have been translated into many different languages and are published all around the world. When she's not writing, she loves collecting vintage fashion and practising the art of fashion illustration. Natasha lives with her husband and three children in Perth, Western Australia.

natashalester.com.au

For Ruby, Audrey and Darcy

CAMILLE

ONE

Patient care: stethoscope whispers, the lubdub of footsteps, huddles of family. And dead minds with beating hearts connecting to live minds with failing hearts.

It all begins with something like a car accident – one's attention unfocussed on the stretch of road ahead, dwelling instead on something that seemed important at the time but which, in hindsight, is not worth giving a life away for. It is usually the passenger – a woman perhaps who had been telling her husband to concentrate on the traffic, to stop being reckless because you never knew what might suddenly appear on the road in front – who comes my way. The husband might have a broken arm, cut face and bruised leg and he feels so guilty about killing his wife that he'll give anything to make up for it. And give he does. Corneas, kidneys, liver, lungs, heart, skin; jigsaw pieces that fit into one body as easily as any other.

Today it's a twenty-year-old woman, Lisa, who fell and cracked her head like Humpty Dumpty while she was rock-climbing. Lisa's mother, Mrs Green, is dipping a fine brush into a pot of ink and tattooing the back of her daughter's hand with a series of gentle and connected curves that look like cells magnified under the lens of a microscope. The words are out of my mouth before I can stop them. 'It's beautiful.'

Mrs Green continues to draw. 'It's permanent ink. It won't come off.'

'Why?'

'You're taking the heart and lungs and eyes that I gave her. So I'm giving her this. Something that can't be taken.'

'The people who receive your daughter's organs know how precious they are.'

She stops painting, lays Lisa's hand on the bed and says, 'Maybe you believe that. Maybe you have to because otherwise you couldn't do what you do. Or maybe you're just saying what you're supposed to say. But what does Lisa get out of it? Nothing. She gives her heart to a stranger who gets out of bed and gets on with their life. Imagine giving away your husband and knowing you'll never get anything back. Is anyone that selfless?'

I nod. '*You* are. And the person who is lucky enough to receive the gift of your daughter's heart won't just get on with their life. They, and their family, will wake up every day and thank you both for being selfless. It's okay to have doubts about what's happening. It's part of the grieving.'

I stop then but my mind doesn't; it's always assessing what I've said, studying the person I'm talking to. It's always trying to think ahead to where the tipping point might be, that invisible point where I have offered either too much or not enough comfort and support and the family change their mind and send their son's or their daughter's or their wife's organs into the crematorium, thus wasting the pieces of them that are still alive.

I pick up Lisa's hand and place it back in her mother's. 'It's nearly time to take her to theatre for the retrieval. Is there anything else you'd like to do with her before that? I can help you to take handprints ...'

Mrs Green cuts in. 'I want to give her a bath.'

Locks of hair, handprints, painted toenails, a change of clothes: these are the usual requests. A bath is not. But a bath it will be. Because a mother is about to watch her daughter be wheeled away to an operating theatre. Her daughter still looks alive. She won't when she comes back.

At the hospital gift shop, I find some soap that smells of flowers rather than disinfectant. I find some clean face washers and a tub of warm water and I take it to Lisa Green's bedside.

Mrs Green looks from her daughter to the props I have assembled and I can see her mind grappling with how something as simple as a bath has now become so difficult – there are tubes and machines and a broken body to navigate.

I pull back the sheets that shroud her daughter. I squeeze some soap into the tub of water and wet the face washer. 'It'll be easier if we start with her feet,' I suggest, knowing that, of all pieces of the body, the feet, being the furthest from the face and the head, are the most depersonalised. There are no tubes to contend with either.

I rub the washer over the top of Lisa's foot, through her toes, around her heel. Mrs Green takes the other washer and copies my actions.

We do not talk as we wash, as our hands and our cloths stroke the scar on Lisa's knee from a childhood accident on a bike perhaps, the line on her thigh where the skin changes from tan to white, the circle of freckles on the back of her right hand. Then her body is clean and there is just her face left to wash. A face that ten minutes ago seemed masked by tape and hidden beneath tubes that snake from mouth to machine. But in the act of washing, those things have receded.

I put the soap down. 'I'll leave you to wash her face.'

'Thank you.' Mrs Green smiles at me and I smile back.

As soon as I open the door at home I hear two voices calling out 'Mama!' Addie runs to me on legs that look like two threads dropping from her hips to the floor. Rosie waddles behind like a plump duck and I think, as I always do, how much Addie, at three years old, looks like Rosie's twin. It is not just because they both have reddish blonde hair and blue eyes; it is because Addie is almost the same size as her eighteen-month-old sister. In fact, they weigh the same; Addie is taller but this is negated by the layer of fat that should sit between her bones and her skin, but doesn't.

'Hi babies.' I bend down and they cuddle against me, one on each side, tucked in close. I kiss their cheeks. 'What did you do today?'

'I painted a flower for you,' says Addie and on hearing

the word paint, Rosie points to the kitchen and runs off, looking back to make sure I'm following her, to show me her work of art.

'It's beautiful,' I say as I look at one piece of paper that is covered with bold slashes of paint in every colour, converging in the centre to a muddy blob of brown, and another paper featuring a lopsided chain of pink semicircles propped up by a green stem.

'Hi Julie.' I smile at the girls' nanny, who is putting away smocks and brushes.

'Hi Camille,' Julie says. 'I've made some chicken and salad for their dinner. Everyone's been good today – nice big sleeps, no problems.'

'Great.' I pick up the paintings and turn back to the girls. 'Let's put these on the whiteboard.'

'Mine first,' shouts Addie, galloping into the playroom.

'Zee-zee!' shrieks Rosie, using her baby-babble version of her name, not wanting to always come second at everything.

I hang both pictures at the same time to avoid the fight that will otherwise occur, pay Julie, go to the toilet with my two shadows – one of whom passes me the toilet paper, the other of whom helps me with my knickers – get changed and then Rosie begins to say, 'Yum-yum-yum.'

'Let's get some dinner, shall we?' and I pick up Rosie and hold Addie's hand as we make our way back to the kitchen and find the food Julie has made. It is all chopped up and set out on plates and I send Julie a text to say thank you, blessing the fact that for two days a week, I do not have to cook.

'Is Daddy coming home?' Addie asks.

'No love, he'll be late tonight.'

I try to remember if Paul has a dinner or a meeting but can't and it doesn't matter anyway because the outcome is the same for me. Work from seven in the morning until five in the evening, home in time to feed the girls their dinner and give Addie her vitamins, to bathe them, read to them and put them to bed. Then do a load of washing, fold the clothes from the last night's load, tidy the kitchen and try to stay awake while I catch up on reading from work. At some stage Paul will come home, reheat his dinner in the microwave and eat while watching CNN. He will put his plate on the kitchen bench, not in the dishwasher, and then he will come upstairs, say, *Hello, how was your day?* before getting back in his car and driving to the pool to swim one kilometre. When he returns, I will be asleep and he will creep into bed beside me, husband and wife, alone together for the first time all day, too tired to care. In the morning I will wake first and stare at him, wondering when I stopped loving my husband.

After the children are in bed and before I get to the pile of newsletters I need to read, my phone rings. It is Sarah, an old friend from uni days.

'How's things?' she asks and I reply, typically, 'Good. You?'

'Busy. Like always. How's Addie?'

'She's good. Still not putting on much weight. But she hasn't been in hospital for a few months.'

'That's good, Camille.' Then there is the inevitable pause

that comes, as it always does in conversations like these, as she tries to work out how to segue gently from the subject of a sick child to something more ordinary.

In the end, she plunges straight in to the subject of her call. 'I'm planning a new exhibition at the gallery.'

'What's it going to be?'

'That depends.'

'On what?' I laugh. 'Is it a mystery I'm supposed to solve?'

Sarah laughs too. 'No. It depends on you.' Then she begins to talk fast, like the Sarah I know, almost intimidating in her eloquence, but also passionate, about art. 'I want to present an exhibition of your father's sculptures. All of the ones influenced by or connected in some way to your mother. I've already started speaking to collectors of his work and they'll loan me the pieces I need. You have the rest.'

I begin to speak but she cuts me off. 'I haven't finished yet. Here's the part I need to talk you into.' She pauses.

'Okay, I'm listening.'

'Actually there are two things I might have to talk you into.'

I can't help but shake my head even though I know Sarah can't see me. 'My mind is flashing back to all the different things you've convinced me to do over the years ... like setting out blankets in the MCA covered with our work and trying to convince the curators that hosting a guerilla-visual-arts cum garage-sale installation was a worthy thing to do.'

Sarah laughs again. 'I'd forgotten about that. But keep thinking along those lines because what I'm about to ask you is nowhere near as bad as that.'

'I feel so much better.'

'I also want to show Jack Darcy's paintings of your mother at the same exhibition. And I want you to curate it.'

All the obvious objections tumble from my mouth. 'Sare, I haven't done anything remotely artistic in years. Not since uni. I'd be a terrible curator. I've been a nurse for too long. My art history degree is, well ... history.'

'Camille, you're the perfect person to curate the exhibition. As well as being Dan and Alix's daughter, your eye for how pieces of art should be connected together is better than mine. You can tell the stories behind the pieces. The stories about Alix and Dan. It's a brilliant idea. At least admit that.'

'It is.' I sigh. 'I won't be able to tell Jack Darcy's stories though.'

'You will. In some way.'

There are so many more objections. Things I should say. *I'm busy at work. What about Addie? I barely have time to live the life I have now, let alone add something else to it.* But then there's the thought of re-examining Dan's sculptures, my father's sculptures, art that I see every day in his studio, the hall of my house, the living room. Of imagining them in an exhibition space, removed from domesticity, placed beside or opposite one of Jack Darcy's paintings. Paintings I have never seen. Paintings I am aware of in the same way I am aware that I haven't had sex with my husband for several months. An unacknowledged fact, better left that way. Because there is safety in the silence of let's-pretend, a safety that allows us to go on living with a minimum of fuss. But there is boredom too. And right now I realise how bored I am with the way domesticity has taken over my life and that this is the first time since having children that I'm excited by something beyond them.

So I say yes.

And then Sarah says, 'By the way, Jack Darcy's agreed to it only on the condition that you meet with him first.'

After I put down the phone I step outside the house, to the studio, my father's studio, and sit at his old work table for a few minutes before going to bed. On top of the table is a photograph of Alix, my mother, a woman painted and sculpted by two men. A muse, then. A Dora Maar. An Edie Sedgwick. Someone shaped from plaster, someone teased to life with a brush. Someone made for others to look upon. And, like all good muses, she was tragic too. One dead husband. Then an unexpected chance to love again before she was dead too.

I have some of the sculptures of Alix. But it is the photograph that captures me now. In it, my mother's hair is majestic; Elizabethan red, it flames down her back. Her features are strong; individually they might be considered ugly, but combined they are striking, like a cocktail you stumble upon in a faraway city and then is never mixed in quite the same way again.

She wears her signature black pencil skirt as well as stockings, black heels – such high heels, she was never afraid of her height – and a blouse of emerald silk with a bow tied at her collar and slightly capped sleeves. A century ago and she would not look out of place, just as she does not look out of place now. A timeless beauty, I once heard someone say and they were right, although the way they meant it was throwaway, clichéd, whereas the way I mean it is that she is always present.

I turn the photograph facedown on to the table so I can no longer see her. But I can still feel – not her – but her absence. It is a tricky thing, this absence. It is somehow tangible, like the photograph, yet I also know that it is not real because neither past nor absence can ever be handled.

Since I was two years old, lack is all I have had of Alix, beside some scant facts: a car, a woman on the road, a tragic accident. All else unspoken.

After Addie was born, and then Rosie, I began to think that the scant facts about my mother were not enough. I worry over them at night, trying to tease the truth out of them, the *what really happened*? But every time I try to recast her out of the remnants of what I was told a long time ago, then this absence, the one thing I have held on to for so long, becomes slipperier. It is no longer a simple loss, something that can be easily explained and understood. It shifts with each question I ask – how can I miss someone I don't know; do I miss *her* or do I miss having a mother; who was she, this infamous Alix; and lastly, did she care for me the way she cared for my father or was death a relief to her rather than a calamity?

Questions that I do not want answered. Questions that I do not want left unanswered.

TWO

I am at work the next day and instead of thinking about grieving families and the organs they have custody of I am studying a piece of paper on which I have written the number Sarah gave me last night. Jack Darcy's. I have dialled it a dozen times and then hung up. Because he is the only one left alive from that time, my mother's time, and he is the only one I care nothing about.

I put the note down on my desk, step out of my office and decide to get some lunch. As I walk past the nurse's station, someone calls out, 'Camille! Phone.'

'Hello.'

'It's Julie. Addie's bleeding. It's everywhere.'

'Have you called the ambulance?'

'Yes.'

'I'll meet them at the children's hospital.'

So. We're back. Or rather, I'm back with Addie. I haven't called Paul and I won't till I know how serious it is. But I'm here, in the ER this time, not that other more frightening acronym, PICU, not yet, waiting. Hoping that whatever it is, this time, does not require a paediatric intensive care unit.

They pull up and I call Paul as soon as I see her. 'Addie's going to PICU.'

'On my way.'

It's nice, I suppose, to not have had to explain. To know that four words are enough. It is a kind of intimacy.

Biliary Atresia. The sound of the words makes me think of sea dragons with their oddly shaped but delicate limbs floating like fronds of leaves through a forest of seagrass, hiding until you get just close enough to see their more deliberate movements. That is not what I thought of when I first heard the words after Addie was born. Then, I thought of witch's fingers probing her liver, finding each bile duct, destroying them, and then wriggling with joy as the bile built up, unable to flow into the intestine, and instead killing off her liver.

The next words were Kasai Procedure, which sounded distinctly more medical. Japanese perhaps, highly technical with a strong scientific pedigree, something to believe in, to trust to fix the problem. And it is Mr Kasai and his procedure that almost made the witch's fingers disappear and the sea dragons take their place. But now they have all failed and we are left with varices: a scarred liver and constricted veins that have weakened and swollen to the point where Addie is vomiting blood. These are the facts that the doctor concentrates on when he explains it to me. Not the ability of a sea dragon to camouflage itself so perfectly within an ocean of weed.

I have just a few moments with Addie after the doctor

leaves and before Paul arrives. I feel like the kin I see at the hospital every day as I hover by her bed, unable to pick her up and hold her and unwilling to resort to the two obvious alternatives, hair-stroking and hand-holding because I know that when she hurts herself, these measures will not stop the tears. I move to lie on the bed beside her, to press my forehead against hers. But Paul comes in and I stop because it is forbidden to lie on a patient's bed in PICU and I want no one to see me break rules that I enforce in my work every day.

Paul walks over to Addie and kisses her cheek. 'Not feeling so good baby?' She doesn't reply of course. She's sedated and transfused with fluid and blood.

So I reply on her behalf. 'It's varices. The cirrhosis is worse. She needs a transplant.'

A transplant. It is simply the process of moving something from one place to another. These are two words we have known, since Addie was born, that we would have to face. Yet we have not, because that kind of conversation requires the closeness of an evening meal for two where we sit side by side and drink champagne, not a half-shouted string of instructions as I run out the door to work or to jog or to visit a gallery; not an always interrupted exchange over a dinner of spaghetti bolognaise where my focus is on cajoling two girls to eat; and not a casual enquiry about one's day as we sit on the sofa at night in the kind of stupor that can only be indulged in once the children are in bed.

Paul's reply is the same as my own to the doctor: nothing. A vast expanse of no words. Because to even start to speak about it is to know that it will never end, that life for some indeterminate time will be governed by something so fickle as the death of another child with a perfect liver and the ability to keep Addie in a space of being sick enough to be near the top of a transplant list but not so sick that she dies of waiting.

Paul falls into a chair and rubs his face with his hands as if that could erase the word *transplant*. He leans forward, elbows on knees, chin held up on both sides by his palms. 'I wanted her to be older when this happened. How soon?'

'She's not critical enough to be at the top of the list.' Best Match, Best Outcome, Most in Need: phrases that I use every day at work. That is how a patient is chosen to be the one lucky enough to receive the too few hearts or lungs or livers that might, through someone else's bad luck, suddenly become available. But these phrases that rule my days do not seem to apply to my daughter; I want to bend the words in some way, to change them, because I know from looking at Addie that she is unlikely to be deemed Most in Need. At this stage.

'How much sicker does she have to be?' Paul asks.

'She'll have an endoscopy when she stabilises. That could cause more bleeding or an infection which would make her a lot sicker.'

'It was a rhetorical question, Camille.'

I know it was, I want to say. And I also want to reach over and pull his hands away from his chin, watch his head jerk forward, shock him into seeing the reality of what a transplant really means. Because how do you explain to a journalist who works with something as pliable as words, who thinks that because he has been through the jaundice, the poor weight gain, the Kasai, the cholangitis, the fevers, the stays in hospital, the IV antibiotics, that he has seen the worst, that this time will be the same as all those other times when he has not and it will not?

I speak to him like a relative at work, small bites of information, not too strong, not too much. 'This is not as bad as it gets. She'll need a liver in the next couple of months.'

'Can she come home?'

'I hope so. But not for a while.'

A code blue is called on another child in PICU. There is a lot of beeping and rushing and shouting. So I move onto the logistics, talk louder than the sounds. 'Someone will need to be with her all the time. We'll need to organise it with work so we can be here in shifts. And be with Rosie as well. She'll feel left out.'

Paul's gaze sweeps the room, as if he has remembered for the first time that he has another daughter. 'Where is Rosie?'

'With Julie. She was with Julie anyway. I was at work today, remember?'

Paul nods briefly, as if not caring about this part of the conversation, so I press on. 'Let me know when you can be here and I'll put it into our diaries so we know when each of us is supposed to be here, when we're supposed to be with Rosie and when we can work. I'll get Julie to work an extra day or two as well.'

Again, the response from Paul is a nod.

I say, in order to stir some kind of action in him, 'We can get Louisa to help. And your mum. And Michelle.'

Paul leaves to call his mother and sister and I wonder why it couldn't be a kidney that she needed, something easier to find, not a liver, which is like searching for one specific piece of salt within the vastness of the ocean.

THREE

'Louisa, it's Camille.'

The woman who raised me, my father's sister, knows straight away that something is wrong.

'What's happened?' she asks.

'It's Addie.' I tell her what's wrong and ask her to help with the bedside roster. She agrees and says, 'Make sure you have some time with Paul too. Otherwise you won't see him, except when you're both flying in and out of Addie's room.'

I try a joke. 'I only see him flying in and out of the house now.'

'You'll need each other.'

That should be true. And I do need him, because I know I can't be by Addie's bed all of the time. I need to look after Rosie too. But when I left him in Addie's room to make my phone calls I did wonder if it would be easier if he was not there, someone else to comfort, someone else to explain things to, someone else to stop me from lying down beside my daughter and tucking her into my arms to make everything better.

I change the subject. 'Sarah called last night. She wants me to curate an exhibition for her. Of Dan's sculptures.'

'What did you tell her?'

'I said yes but I think I should tell her I can't. Not with Addie getting worse like this.'

'Do you want to do it?'

I pause and remember how I had felt last night when I spoke to Sarah. Like a child learning to crawl, stretching out for an object placed just beyond reach. Understanding for the first time how it might feel to inch forward and grasp it. Knowing that if I pushed a little harder, I probably could. 'Yes. I really do.'

Louisa laughs. 'So you just need me to tell you it's okay to do it. To tell you that you're not abandoning your sick child in her hour of need.'

I laugh too. 'Something like that.' Then I stop laughing and say, 'I just want something more than damaged bodies and shitty nappies and squabbles about never being home in time for dinner. I want something fine. Like ... I don't know ...' I scrabble around in a mind that has fallen out of the habit of such discussion. 'Like falling in love. That's what the exhibition should be about.'

'Sounds like you've thought about it too much to say no.'

I realise Louisa is right. As usual. And then it slips out. 'The exhibition's a joint one. With Jack Darcy's paintings of Alix as well.'

Louisa pauses and then her words almost shock me. 'That's a love story too, Camille.'

'How can you be so generous?' I blurt. 'Dan was your brother.'

'Dan was dead, Camille. And Alix grieved too much. Until

Jack came along. She needed him. Because she had you and you can't raise a child with grief.'

I wonder if that is true. If I am raising my own children with grief, an insidious grief that is all the more dangerous for being unsaid. Because it is for a loss that hasn't yet happened, a loss that might not happen. A loss that we have simply been threatened with, ever since Addie was born. And grief over another loss, one I have never quite understood. That of my mother.

I shake my head and say, 'Jack Darcy wants to meet me.'

'I think it would be good for you to meet him.'

'I'm not so sure.'

After I speak to Louisa, I call work and repeat the story about Addie, organising to drop back from two shifts a week to one. Of course they have to say yes; how can they refuse a mother with a critically ill child? But I can hear them thinking, thoughts that I share, that at one shift a week there is barely any point working.

Since having the children I can see why so many mothers give up. It is too hard. Babysitting arrangements fall apart like torn skin, children become ill every month and never at the same time and want only their mother at home with them.

But to be nothing except a mother and Paul's wife is to be nothing at all.

Paul and I decide that I should be the one to go home to Rosie. Addie is sedated and is unlikely to wake up for hours whereas

Rosie has seen her sister vomiting blood and taken away in an ambulance.

'I'm home,' I call, as usual, and, as usual, there is the sound of running feet but it is only one little girl, Rosie, who appears at the door, falling over in her rush, let down by chubby eighteen-month-old legs that don't quite perform with the skill she demands.

'Mummy,' she cries as she jumps straight up from her crash-landing and grabs my legs, wrapping both arms tightly around my knees. 'Cuddle!'

I bend down and pick her up, kissing her juicy cheeks, then I walk into the kitchen where Julie is packing up her things.

'How's she been?' I ask.

'Not too bad. A bit whiny. Asking for you. She knows something's wrong.'

'Whereabouts ...' I start to ask, looking around the room but Julie interjects and says, 'She was lying on her little couch. It was covered in,' she pauses and looks at Rosie, 'you know, so I threw it in the bin and cleaned up the floor.'

'Did Rosie see?'

'Not at first. Addie was tired so I got her some books and she sat down to read. Rosie was playing with the blocks. But she came running over when Addie started crying. She saw enough.'

'Thanks for cleaning it all up. You didn't have to.'

Julie shrugs. 'I didn't mind. How is she?'

Rosie begins to tug at my hair, bored now, wanting me all to herself, wanting Julie gone now that I am home. 'Not great,'

I say as I try to disentangle myself from Rosie's fists. Rosie begins to flap, not wanting to let go of my hair now that she has my attention.

Julie smiles. 'I'll go. Give Addie a big kiss for me, Rosie-Posie.'

Rosie shakes her head and says, 'No.' Nothing, not even a sick sister, can stop the incessant no-ing of an eighteen month old. Then Rosie smiles and waves her fat fingers at Julie. As Julie closes the door, Rosie wriggles out of my arms and onto the floor. She runs off down the hall to Addie's room and says, 'Addie?'

So we sit on Addie's bed together, Rosie cushioned in my lap, and I take out the book we all made together, which has pictures of Addie in the hospital, pictures cut from newsletters showing doctors with stethoscopes caring for patients and a picture of us all home together at the end.

I read her the story we have created about Addie, who has a bad fairy inside her liver. The bad fairy is casting a spell to make Addie sick. Then a doctor magically appears one night and uses her special wand-shaped tools to take out Addie's liver, bad fairy and all. The doctor gives Addie a brand new liver, which in our book has been coloured in bright pink by Rosie and has a bow tied around it in festive red. The bad fairy is turned into a sea dragon by the doctor, and is made to swim out into the ocean where spells are drowned before they can be cast. The sea dragon eventually decides that she is sorry for what she has done and sends Addie a magic shell which will stop her from getting sick ever again. Everybody lives happily ever after.

Every time I read it I can't help but wonder if we will have to write another book about what happens when the doctor can't find the bad fairy and so, instead of becoming a sea dragon, she turns into a hooded spinster on a boat, taking children away to a secret place from which they can never return because they are lost in sleep. It is a story without precedent in their Disneyfied lives. Sleeping Beauty, Snow White; these girls are all awoken from sleep in the end and their princes destroy the bad fairies and wicked witches. How do they believe in a story where the simple act of waking becomes impossible?

I put the book away and make some burritos for dinner. Rosie picks at her food and I do not bother to play aeroplanes or sing songs or threaten her with no dessert because one poor dinner will not kill a child, not today. Then I run the bath and she laughs when I let her splash water everywhere so that my hair is dripping and I end up taking off my clothes and hopping in the bath with her. She tips cups of water over my head and pretends to wash my hair, she jabs her fingers at my nipples as if she expects them to squeak or beep like a plastic toys and then she sits still and serious and intrigued as I blow-dry her hair and mine.

We read *Addie Versus the Bad Fairy* five times over; even Maisy Mouse has lost her charm in the face of such a story. Then it is time for bed.

'Addie,' she says to me again as I zip her into her sleeping bag.

'Let's blow her a kiss all the way to the hospital,' I say. 'Ready?'

Rosie nods and we kiss and puff into the air with all our might, listening until we are certain we can hear the faint sound of Addie plucking the kisses from the air and sticking them to her cheeks.

Then I kiss Rosie's cheeks and her forehead and her chin, just like Addie does to her every night before bed.

But it is not enough. She tucks her head into my shoulder and starts to whinge. 'Addie. Addie. Addie.'

'She'll be home soon,' I lie.

I close Rosie's door, go outside and walk straight across the lawn to my father's studio. I slap my feet against the path, driving out the anger and the sadness and the frustration before it can turn to tears.

I sit and turn on my laptop and then type an email to Jack Darcy instead of calling him. My fingers batter the keyboard, then I skim over my words.

Dear Jack, I can meet you on Friday at noon during my lunch break. If we could meet somewhere near the hospital, that would suit me best. Camille.

There is no need for introductions. He knows who I am in the same way that I am very aware of who he is. So I press send and then I take out a notebook and pen. I push into the paper, nearly tearing it, and after I have written *Dan's Sculptures* at the top of a page, I underline it twice in a gesture that looks like a flourish but is more of an assault. At the top of another page I write *Jack's Paintings*; my pen is not so harsh now because lists are a way to organise things, a way to think of something other than my child and her dying liver. I can be a curator for an hour or so until it is time to go back and sit with Addie.

But I need a theme or an idea first. I remember that from my uni days. Something to coalesce the exhibition, otherwise it is just a motley collection of pieces, strung together like mismatched jewels on a rusty chain. What if things have changed, though, in the intervening years? What if themes are obsolete in this digital age? I feel sure that postmodernism must have passed us by but I have no idea what it has been replaced with.

Falling in love, I had said to Louisa; that was what the exhibition should be about. Because that perpetuates the legend I have grown up with – that Alix and Dan shared a grand and glorious love for too short a time before he was stolen away by Death. Then somehow, impossibly, Alix found Jack and fell with him into the same kind of love, that which you surrender to, utterly.

Or did she? That is always the question I have wanted to ask but who can you ask such a thing of when there is no one left alive? Except Jack.

I reach across to the phone, to call Sarah, to tell her I cannot do this. I'm an impostor who has nothing to say about her father's art, who has nothing to say about her mother's lover's art. As my arm moves, it knocks a postcard that I keep propped up on the desk; it is of a bronze sculpture by Camille Claudel, sculptor, Rodin's lover, the woman whose name my father wanted to give me before he even knew I existed and which was, in the end, given to me by my mother.

The bronze is called *The Waltz*. It was my father's favourite sculpture. Two figures clasp one another, dancing, heads bowed together, their legs a drapery of fabric. They seem on the one hand precarious, as if their absorption in dancing with one another might cause them to topple over. But to look at their hands and their necks is to discover otherwise. The grip of their hands speaks of their strength together more clearly than if they were to come alive and declare it to the viewer. And Claudel has sculpted their necks so that these pieces of their bodies say more than any pair of eyes ever could about desire; their necks are like tentacles of yearning. They float together, unbalanced but in no danger of collapse, rapt, entranced, unrecoverable.

I hold the postcard against my chest and look back across to the house through a distortion of tears, to the lit-up but empty living room and I want to put everybody in there together, beneath the lights: my mother and father, Paul and me, caught in a waltz, and the girls, Rosie and Addie, holding hands and galloping in circles between us, laughing, nearly tripping but never falling, under our feet but not in the way.

The love that we all should have for one another dances beside us. Then waltzes away.

When I was in love with my husband, I used to dream about other men, men from work mostly, men who were good-looking but who I wasn't necessarily attracted to. In my dreams I would be naked, in a chair perhaps, my breasts much bigger than they are in reality, and the man from work would be sucking my clitoris and rubbing my nipples and I would be arching back, pushing my pelvis into him, deeper into his mouth, harder against his tongue and then I would come, quickly, freely. Now that I no longer love my husband I dream about him, not about men I barely know, and it is my husband making me come like that, when we are both asleep at night. I do not set out to dream about him; he creeps into my head at about two in the morning and after those nights, when I wake up, I feel content, loved, at peace. It doesn't last beyond the cry of the baby and me rolling out of bed to shower.

Then Paul's car pulls into the drive; my turn to sit by Addie's bed, his turn to be at home. I put the postcard down, blow my nose, wipe my eyes and go back into the house.

The next day, Addie is still sedated. I'm rostered on at work so I keep my shift and Louisa agrees to sit with Addie. I drop Rosie at her Aunt Michelle's on the way.

Within minutes of arriving, I get a call from the intensivist. There is a brain-dead twenty-five-year-old male in ICU. Jumped drunk into the river and drowned. I check the organ donor registry. He's not on it. I relay the information back to the intensivist. 'I'll call you back after I've spoken to the family,' he says.

This time we're lucky. The family bring up organ donation with the intensivist first. I don't stop for the next twelve hours.

There are tests to organise: chest X-ray, ECG, bloodwork. I contact the heart, liver and pancreas transplant teams and give them the twenty-minute warning for the teleconference. They dial in at 10.15 a.m. precisely. They've each narrowed down their lists to two or three people. I organise the cross-matching of blood at the Red Cross. Probably only one of the three potential heart transplant recipients will turn out to be negative on cross-match and that's the deciding factor. The other two will never know how close they came to getting a new heart.

Once the bloods come back, I book the theatres for the retrieval teams because now I know who the recipients are and how far they have to travel to get their last chance at life. All the time I'm helping the ICU nurses care for the patient and checking in with the family. Everything is going so well I almost cannot believe it. Then I go back to the patient's bed to see if there is anything the family need.

The man's mother has her head bent over her son's hands as if she is praying. 'I'm sorry,' I say as I turn around. 'I'll come back later.'

She looks up and smiles at me. 'I was thinking about the person who'll get his heart. I've heard that they say their personality changes. They become like the person who gave them the heart. Maybe this way a bit of my son stays alive.'

I don't reply but she wants me to so she prods me, 'You must have heard the stories?'

'I have.' It is important that I offer no opinion, no judgement, even though that is what she wants. Because who really believes in spirits, in ghosts, in a transparent, flying being that exists between a person's life and death, that occupies other bodies and dreams and private spaces? No, there is a person, and then there isn't. That is all. Her son will not be reincarnated through the beating of his heart in another person's body.

She reads my disbelief into my noncommittal reply. 'You don't believe it.'

'We can pass on a letter from you to the people who receive his organs and they may reply. Many people find this helps.' I know, right then and there, that she will do this. That she will form a maternal relationship with a complete stranger through her son's heart. She will become a donor mother to the person who receives her son's heart, even if he is a man fifteen years older than she is. She will become part of a peculiar fictional relationship that she will tend with the same intensity as she tended her bond with her son.

I am not expecting her next question. 'Why do you do this job?' she asks.

'My mother was a heart transplant surgeon. One of the first. She cared for the almost-dead, spent all her time trying to keep them alive, but she watched many of them die. Because she never had enough hearts. So I do this job for the almost-dead patients. That's what my mother called them.'

'If they're almost dead then what is he?' She points to her son. 'He looks alive but he's not. He's brain-dead, so they tell me, but his heart's beating. He's almost-dead too.'

No, he's just dead, I think. But I don't say this. I believe it though. Because how else could I do my job?

I am saved from answering by his blood pressure alarm sounding and I begin to administer vasopressors while the

ICU nurse organises a heated blanket because his body temperature is also dropping.

Later, I sit with his mother and father while the retrieval surgery takes place. We don't talk a lot, except when I go to the theatre to get updates, which I then relay to them. His organs are perfect, beautiful, full of life, I tell them. He has saved so many lives. Everyone is so grateful. Yes, he is dead now; his heart is gone.

They cry some more when it is finished, when he is finished, at last, in their eyes. It is hard for them to leave. So I embrace them and call them a cab and send them home because otherwise they will sit here all night, not quite grieving, and not quite believing.

Then I go back and find the ICU nurse. It is midnight now but it was her first organ donor case and she is, as expected, in tears. So I debrief with her, because she is used to trying to keep people alive in ICU; she is a critical care nurse and caring is what she does. She is not used to having to keep alive someone who is already dead. I make her a coffee, pass her tissues and embrace her too before she leaves.

At last it is my turn to leave. I go straight to a different hospital. My daughter's hospital. I hand Paul a coffee, then send him home without an embrace.

As I sit by Addie's bed, I remember what Mrs Green had said just the other day about giving my husband away. I look at Addie lying here and I know that if I could put Paul in her place, I would.

FOUR

I scan the ICU: beds of children who cannot move or speak or cry out, parents who can and do cry out, and worse, beds with children whose parents have gone home and left them there, alone.

I pull my chair right next to Addie's bed and talk to her about Rosie and how we have made cupcakes with purple icing for her when she wakes. 'I know you won't be able to eat them,' I say, tucking her hair behind her ear and out of the way of her closed eyes, 'but Rosie really wanted to make them for you. I'll put a couple in the freezer for you and you can have them when you come home.' *When you come home.* If I say it aloud, then it will happen.

The parents of the little boy in the bed next to Addie's look across at me as I speak, and I can tell, by the terror in their eyes, that this is their first time in ICU. That it is a kind of nightmare they have not settled into: a tube-covered child surrounded by sixteen other tube-covered children, some of whom may die or have died while they wait for their own child to live.

I smile at them but they look away, ashamed to have been

caught looking at another mother and child, comparing, perhaps, whose child looks worse off, hoping it is not their child who does. Because that is what you do in ICU; you have no sympathy left for anyone else and you think thoughts that you could never imagine yourself thinking in a park on a sunny afternoon – that you draw hope from a child who appears sicker than your own.

I lean back in my chair as Addie's nurse conducts her checks. 'Are you going down to the hostel tonight?' she asks and I shake my head.

'I'll stay here.'

'They're not going to lift her sedation until tomorrow. You should get some sleep.'

'I'll sleep when she's better.'

'I'll get someone to bring you some water.'

'Thanks.'

And then I do what I have learned, over the past three years, to do. To close off the machines and parents and children by putting on a pair of imaginary blinkers that narrow my sight to Addie. I kiss her cheek and tell her to have sweet dreams about going to the park and feeding the turtles when she comes home. And then I take two notebooks out of my handbag. The first is plain and black and contains nothing other than the two headings I scratched on its pages the night before: *Dan's Sculptures* and *Jack's Paintings*. I turn to a new page and crease it back, firmly. At the top I write: *Notes on an Exhibition.*

The other book has a red and gold fabric cover; it is bound

with ribbon. I have taken it out of a box containing my mother's possessions, possessions I have previously only glanced over, noting that there were letters and diaries and clothes, but never reading or unfolding anything. Because, as well as possessions, the box contains whispers from long ago. Louisa's voice on the telephone on the night my mother died, overheard by me because I had been woken by a bad dream about an angel with black wings cutting through the floor beneath my bed.

'Jack,' Louisa had said that night. 'What do I tell Camille?'

But perhaps I have invented this as an excuse not to look into the box – I was only two at the time so how can I possibly remember that conversation, spoken beneath the breath, like a secret?

I look down at the book in my hand, the one from my mother's box; the contradiction between the unspoiled ribbon and the used pages suggests a thing of importance. And the red on the cover seems too brazen a colour for the things I do not know.

As I begin to read, I want to slap the covers closed. Because the first pages are an account of the first time my mother slept with my father and it seems that she has documented the encounter with the same accuracy that she would use to record the particulars of a patient's condition.

But after the first few words it is almost as if I am a child again, back in my bed at Louisa's house, hearing her stories about a woman who is called my mother and a man who is called my father but of whom I have no recollection.

Midnight would often find me, a girl who could not sleep,

standing outside the door to Louisa's room waiting until she heard the tiny squeaks of my mouth sucking the ends of my hair. She would gently remove the wet strands of hair from between my lips and guide me back to my room, all the while saying, 'If we tuck you in properly, this time you'll be able to sleep.'

Then she would make a great show of folding my knees up to my chin and wrapping my arms around my legs so I looked like a nautilus shell beached on white blankets. She would plump the quilt and shroud it over my body before lying down beside me. And on nights when I could not stop myself from sucking so hard on my hair that I ground the ends of it between my teeth I would say, 'Tell me about my mum and my dad.'

And as she began to talk I wouldn't even notice when my hair fell out of my mouth and my eyes began to close because I was listening to a fairytale with real people who had real names – Alix and Dan, not Snow White or Cinderella. Louisa always called them by their names when she told me stories about them; she didn't say *your Mum* and *your Dad* and that suited me fine because then Alix and Dan could be the storybook characters they were rather than the Mum and Dad they could not be.

I put Alix's diary on the table beside me. It is not an account of the first time she had sex with my father. It is an account of how they began, the two of them, and as I read it I find it hard to separate Alix and Dan from the art she describes; she is an artifice fixed in plaster yet here again, in her own words, she seems make-believe.

I place my own notebook and pen on my lap. I know what I want to do for the exhibition. I want to fit Louisa's stories and Alix's diaries around the sculptures, around the paintings, and then connect their words to what I think I know: the whispers, the secrets, the words that are lost on the sighs of exhaled breath. I want to write about more than the woman I've been led to believe in, the woman caught in plaster and paint: Alix-the-subject, Alix-the-romantic-and-tragic-heroine, Alix-the-muse.

Notes on an exhibition, I will call them. An exhibition of sculpture and painting. An exhibition of a life. I will give some of the notes to Sarah. I will keep some for myself.

NOTES ON AN

EXHIBITION

A WOMAN SHOUTING, SILENTLY
(Plaster, 7 x 8cm. Originally titled *Open Mouth* but re-named by the artist after its first exhibition.)

Alix – my mother – met Dan – my father – at an exhibition of his sculptures. And, as coincidence would have it, Alix met her lover, Jack Darcy, at an exhibition of my father's work too, albeit some time later.

A friend of Alix's invited her to the opening of an exhibition by an up-and-coming sculptor. Alix had gone along to the show because she liked free champagne and smoked salmon bites, not because she had any interest in art.

She noticed the sculptor being double-cheek-kissed and back-patted by women wearing pastel Chanel, women whose hands were stacked with rings like an abacus. He smiled at the Chanel women – too nicely, Alix thought, because surely an artist should be more cynical about such whimsical patronage. She was sure the Chanel suits and overringed fingers wouldn't be around if he was just another poor artist starving in whatever sufficed for a garret during those postmodern days of the early eighties.

Then, rather than study him, she'd studied his work. He'd used plaster – a material she'd only ever thought of as a healer of broken bones – to make sculptures of bodies, or not even bodies, but parts of bodies. Body parts not quite broken yet not quite whole. A set of toes without a foot, for instance. A knee, sitting alone, so that it didn't appear to be a knee, as if it needed the context of shin and thigh to make it be a knee. And a mouth, all thin stretched lips and openness as if it were struck to death whilst shouting.

Alix had been staring at that mouth, really staring, she knew, so that she hadn't even noticed him step up beside her.

'What do you think she's saying?' he asked.

'Something no one wants to hear,' Alix replied, then shrugged at the sound of her thoughts accidentally voiced. 'You're the artist; what did you want her to say?'

'Maybe she's saying yes to the man who's asking her out to dinner tomorrow night.' He smiled at her. 'Are you free?'

'Well,' Alix hesitated, 'as she seems to have lost her voice, I'll have to step in and say ... yes.'

The night of her date with Dan, Alix stood in front of the mirror wearing a shirt and knickers, wondering what she should wear to dinner with an artist who, according to her friend, had made at least one hundred thousand dollars on opening night by selling plaster body pieces to the women in Chanel suits.

Everything in her wardrobe seemed too plain or conservative or clinical even, so Alix took out the blow-dryer and concentrated on her hair instead of her clothes, examining the colour as each section began to dry. She wouldn't allow herself to be considered a redhead – although others often described her as such – because her hair was really a motley orange colour, like ripe mangoes. It was this orangeness that she would like to get away from.

She was sure that her life would have been different if she'd had distinctly red hair. Redheads were showgirls, dancers or queens. Unfettered jobs with irregular hours, irregular pay and a certain attitude. A redhead would have been to Africa instead of just talking about it. A redhead would have bought the Bvlgari necklace she saw every day in the window of the shop down the road because a redhead would not have to worry about whether it would offend the eyes of the relatives of the almost-dead everyday at work.

Alix finished blow-drying her hair so that it sat in a sleek, smooth line at the bottom edge of her shoulder blades. She turned away from the mirror. Besides, none of her patients would trust her if she had properly red hair. They'd think of other women, shape-shifters, whose red hair foreshadowed their deviousness – Orlando, Ophelia, Elizabeth – because red was a fluid colour even at the same time as it was strong. It was the colour of scalded skin; it was the colour of love in a clichéd heart.

'Congratulations,' Alix said as she slipped into the seat beside him at the bar.

Dan put a glass of champagne in front of her. 'Hope you like champagne. It's all I've drunk for the last twenty-four hours. It's not too often your show gets described in the *Herald* as the best of the year.'

Alix took a sip from her glass. 'So you're drunk and arrogant. Fun date.'

He looked at her for a moment then said, 'I'm neither. Just truthful. But yes, it should be a fun date.'

Alix ran her finger through the ring of water droplets left by her glass on the surface of the bar. She glanced at him. He was tall and blond and blessed. So she chinked her glass against his and said, 'To a fun date.'

He smiled, finished his drink and moved his body closer to hers. And there it was. A shiver of skin, like breeze drifting through the night of her dreams.

'So what do you do when you're not going to art shows or out with arrogant artists?' Dan said.

'I'm a surgeon.' Alix knew that information often ended such conversations. It wasn't feminine enough. Men seemed to prefer nursing, or teaching perhaps.

But he asked the next logical question. 'What kind?'

'I'm with the new heart transplant unit at St Vincent's.'

'I'd love to watch you do one.' He grinned. 'Now I sound weird.'

'It's not the kind of thing men ordinarily want to watch me do.'

He laughed. 'I mean for my sculpture. I like body parts.'

She finished her drink. 'Whole bodies too, I hope.'

Alix went to Dan's studio after dinner. Although, she thought, 'studio' was a word too poetic to describe the triangular attic at the top of his flat. It had very little furniture, just an armchair and a desk. Most of the space was taken up with white figures, like the ones she had seen at the exhibition the previous night.

'Plaster breathes,' Dan said, taking her hand and placing it along the torso of a figure of a woman.

Alix felt moistness beneath her fingers, a dampness rising like sweat from the white rock.

'It takes the moisture from the air,' he continued. 'That's why I like to work with it. It's not lifeless.'

Dan's hand traced her fingers, which rested still on the plaster woman. 'But if the moisture in the air disappears, she begins to desiccate. To thirst. And then she becomes too fragile to shape.' He touched Alix's arm, then her collar bone, the middle of her chest, and stopped to rest at her belly button.

To turn around? To move? To stay where she was? Before she could decide, he lifted the hem of her skirt and moved his hand up along her thigh; he found the top of her knickers and slid his hand inside, over the thin line of hair on her pubic bone. Then he traced a path downwards, pressing lightly, circling around and around, increasing the pressure by the slightest increments until Alix felt her legs part because he wasn't pressing firmly enough nor circling quickly enough and so she began to move backwards and forwards against his hand, to rub, hard, and she came just as his other hand found her nipple and his mouth tasted the skin along the back of her neck.

Six months later there was a wedding, a house in Elizabeth Bay for the now famous and wealthy sculptor and his heart-surgeon wife, and a year or so of bliss.

CAMILLE'S HEAD

(Plaster, 13 x 11cm. The only piece from this time that is not of the artist's wife.)

Bliss. For Alix, it was the kind of bliss she had always imagined Cinderella and her prince must have shared in their happy ever after, the sort of bliss that came after the full stop, that was never written about because it was too private and also indescribable – how could something as simple as words on paper be capable of depicting this?

Take their honeymoon. Europe of course. Gorging on art. And then the discovery of a small gallery down a lane into which they had only ventured because they were lost, but didn't care because what greater delight was there than to be lost beneath the sun in Florence with the person you loved, holding hands, kissing, desiring, finding your way out only because then you could do more than kiss, more than run hands beneath the backs of shirts, more than feel one another through a filter of clothing.

Dan had seen the sign over Alix's shoulder. 'Another gallery?' he asked and she shrugged, not caring enough to say either yes or no.

But, walking inside the gallery is a scene Alix will remember later, when Dan lies dying, and she will understand that they were not lost, that something, fate if you will, had made them turn down that lane and into that gallery, the walls of which were hung with masks. Death masks.

Alix didn't understand what she was seeing at first until Dan told her. 'Some are made from plaster,' he said, indicating the far wall, 'and these ones are made from wax.'

Alix moved in close, so close that she could see or imagine, she wasn't sure which, the faintest etchings of the fine hair that covers a person's cheeks. 'It looks like the wax is lit up from behind,' she said.

'Wax soaks up light,' Dan said. 'See how the skin looks almost moist.'

'Yes.' Alix paused. 'Some of these faces look more alive than the people I treat in the hospital every day.' She looked up at Dan. 'When I see things like this I wonder what being dead really means. The moment I take out someone's heart on the operating table, they're dead, really – a machine is keeping them alive until I can stitch in a new heart. But I look at this mask and it's a person. I can almost feel them breathing. If his wife walked into this gallery and saw his face here on the wall she'd think he was still living, surely?'

'They used to take death masks of unidentified bodies. That way, if someone came looking for a missing person, they could view the death mask and see if it was the person they were searching for.'

'What about just to keep someone with you, forever? A mask is more reliable than memory, more immediate than a photograph.'

Dan stepped closer, ran the backs of his fingers across her cheekbone. 'Are you saying you'd need a mask to remember me after I died?'

'You're not allowed to die. Ever. Besides, I'm a heart surgeon. I can fix anything that goes wrong.'

The house in Elizabeth Bay straddled their two worlds of real bodies and plaster bodies. The hospital was just a short drive away and Dan had a studio built, separate from the house, at the back of the garden.

He worked when she worked and so their life worked, perfectly. If she was called in at midnight then he would get up too, go to the studio and sculpt until she returned home. Then they would cook breakfast together – always bacon and eggs, mushrooms and toast because working at midnight made them both ravenous. Then they would collapse into bed in a flurry of arms and legs and hips and backs before finally falling asleep, waking whenever it suited them to go out for dinner or to a gallery. He sustained her, made it possible for her to work twenty hours straight at the hospital because he did the same, they did everything the same; sometimes Alix forgot that there had ever been a time before Dan.

Then there would be a few days when she would work normal hours. Go to work at seven in the morning, come home at seven in the evening and not be on call at night. She loved those days, loved stepping into their house and feeling the warmth – Dan always kept the heater on high and so Alix only ever wore T-shirts, even in winter – but she cherished the fact that he did because when she opened the door and felt the rush of hot air, that was when she knew she was home. The house smelt warm too; the ginger tea that he drank with the commitment of a caffeine addict fragranced the air, as did the pot of soup he'd reheated for lunch, or the vegetables he'd roasted for dinner. And the wall in the hall that he'd insisted on painting amber did have the effect he'd said it would – she'd thought of Betadine when she first saw the colour – but when it was finished and every time she came home she thought of welcomes and friends and drinks and Louisa. Then there was him. Dan. She could feel the heat of his art, his inspiration, scalding the air, could almost see it firing on his skin. She could hear it too, in the rasp crackling over plaster, the fall of dust onto the floor.

She tried hard to understand his world – the slurry of white paste and the way he transformed it into art, working away on it long after she thought it was finished, until he'd made it into something more than she could have ever imagined it would be – because he was the only person who understood Alix's world. She would often take him into the hospital late at night and show him things, because who else could she talk to – the only woman in a team of alpha males.

She took him up to the roof where she had stood for the first time as a surgical resident, watching the row of green traffic lights and the two police cars, sirens slicing into the quiet of night, speed to the hospital with a heart on ice in an esky in the boot. She told him how she felt as she raced down the stairs to tell the surgical team that the heart had arrived, intoxicated with the thought of the power she might have one day as the surgeon stitching in the heart, rather than being, as she was then, so inferior as to be often overlooked, happy to have been given a job – even one as lowly as being the runner on the stairs – and not fighting for once to be that most impossible thing – a female hoping to be a heart surgeon.

Occasionally, Alix would take Dan into the anatomy lab at the hospital late in the evening when she knew the interns would be gone. She introduced him to her cadaver, the one she practised on every day, knowing she had to be more than perfect if she wanted to be a heart transplant surgeon – she had to be peerless.

The cadaver was a man, aged about forty she guessed, slightly overweight, covered in hair and sporting a curly black mullet on his head. A man whose heart she knew better than anyone's.

Dan jumped when she snapped on the lights in the lab and she laughed. 'They're all well and truly dead, especially now that they've had interns hacking into them every day. They're not about to leap up and tickle your neck.'

As she finished speaking her hand crept up and brushed his neck. He jumped again, then grabbed her hand, laughed, pulled her towards him and stopped. 'I don't think I can kiss you in front of dead people,' he whispered.

'You don't have to whisper, they definitely can't hear you.'

He smiled. 'Maybe if I pretend that this is a studio and the bodies are sculptures or something.'

Alix unzipped a white body bag on a trolley and nodded. 'They are sculptures. As a surgeon I get to find the beauty in them that no one else sees. Like the thinness of the wall of his atrium. If it tears, you die. But mostly it doesn't. I have an old T-shirt that's about the same thickness and it's full of holes.'

Dan stepped up beside her and Alix could see that he had become used to the smell of formalin, that his eyes were no longer focussed on the tattoo of a butterfly that sat in the middle of the man's chest, asserting the fact that he was once a person, an individual who chose, for a particular reason, to have a butterfly drawn between his lungs.

'Show me,' Dan said and his face had become the one he wore when he was working, the expression in his eyes that of a concentrated dream.

Alix took his hand, just as he had done in his studio the night of their first date. She pulled back the incised skin, lifted out the pre-cut ribcage and plunged his gloved fingers into the opened thorax. She moved his hand as she spoke. 'Here are the four chambers of the heart: right atria, left atria, right ventricle, left ventricle.'

She stopped moving his hand, looked up at him and continued. 'I like the word chamber. It makes me think of bedchamber, a private space, a lovely space. Just like the heart. The filling and pouring and looping of blood, the relaxation and contraction that must all occur, that usually does occur, in sequence, in perfect time over forty million beats a year.'

Dan ran his hand over the surface of the heart. 'What does it feel like to touch a heart that's still working?'

Dan was the only person she knew who would ask, who would think of such a thing. She leaned over and kissed him, reflecting on how unromantic the situation should be – two people with their hands stuck in a dead man's chest – and almost laughed. Then she answered him. 'In surgery you get to feel what it is that makes a person alive.'

For the first time in her life, it occurred to Alix that the feeling was similar to love.

'Let's have a baby.' Dan said this to Alix one night as she stepped into his studio, expecting to see what he'd been working on all day but seeing instead the grin that always made her lean in to him so that her lips were right there, waiting to taste the air into which his words would fall.

She laughed. How could he be serious? How could their life, their crazy, awake-at-all-hours, eat-when-you-can and almost-never-sleep existence accommodate a baby?

'I mean it,' he said, drawing a circle with his finger over her belly. 'I want to feel a baby kicking my hand. I want to watch over your shoulder while you feed the baby. I'll sculpt you both.' He laughed. 'But there isn't a plaster strong enough to hold in it all the love that I'll feel. I tried though.'

And Alix's eyes moved to the sculpture he was indicating, one she'd never seen before and which he must have worked at furiously all day, because it was finished, or so she thought.

It was the head of a baby, Dan's imagined image of his child before he even knew that he would be a father, because he never knew that he would be a father. The sculpture was small, the size of a ball, but finely detailed – half-closed eyes, waxy newborn skin, an imperfectly shaped skull, a searching mouth.

That night, in the studio with Alix, he named the baby Camille, even though Camille was just a dream.

LIFE/DEATH

(Plaster, 75 x 35cm. Part of a series called *Transformation*.)

When she was a medical student and before she met Dan, Alix had sometimes imagined, in a kind of immature, Hollywood-style movie fantasy, that someone she loved would declare to her that they were dying. In her imaginings, upon receiving such news, she would be stoic, an unattractive word, reminiscent of dowagers with unwaxed moustaches on their stiff upper lips but perfectly suited to the way she would respond. Because, in her eyes, another death brought with it another harvest. Time to cut. To plant. To grow.

But then, at half-past eight on a Tuesday night over dinner at a restaurant, Dan told Alix he was dying. Stoicism was the furthest thing from her mind.

There was nothing surprising about the way Alix's week had begun. On the Monday, for instance, she had begun an ICU rotation and was working with donors rather than recipients for six weeks to see the other side of the transplant equation. The frustrating side. Especially when, as now, a family withdrew their consent to donation at the last minute because the wife was no longer convinced that her husband was dead.

'I thought you died when your heart stopped. That's what death used to be,' the wife had said to Alix at the hospital.

'Technically, that's true,' Alix had replied. 'The Harvard criteria for certification of brain death have only been around since 1968 ...'

'My husband's heart is still beating.'

'But his brain is no longer functioning. If we turn off the machines that are breathing for him, his heart will stop.'

'You mean his heart will be beating when you cut him open and take it out.'

'Yes. But he won't feel anything. He has no brain activity ...'

'He always followed his heart. Always believed in heart over mind. He'll feel it. I can't give you his heart. Or anything else.'

'Technically, hearts can't feel.'

At this point the intensivist had stepped in and asked Alix to leave because she wasn't supposed to harangue the kin of brain-dead patients for their organs. As Alix turned away, she saw the wife lay her hand on her husband's chest and smile.

Alix was thinking about that conversation when she arrived home. She went straight to Dan's studio, as was her custom, wincing at the noise of his rasp filing away at the plaster sculpture.

'What do you think?' he asked.

She walked around the piece, seeing it from all sides. It was a woman with a hole right through the upper left section of her chest. In the woman's hand was a strawberry with a bite taken out of it.

Alix leaned in. On closer inspection, she could see that it was not a strawberry; the woman was holding her heart in her hand and the bitten piece was in her mouth. The woman was smiling and Alix thought, she hasn't felt any pain.

'I'm not sure what it means,' Alix said.

'I don't have a particular metaphor in mind,' he said.

She frowned. 'So why did you sculpt it?'

He wiped the dust off his hands and moved over to hug her, to kiss her mouth. 'She's you. I'm doing a series about death. She's the centrepiece. Transforming death into life.'

'That's not what I did today.' Alix stretched out her hand and then withdrew it. She wanted to touch the plaster woman but wasn't sure whether that would damage her. So she said, 'She doesn't look dead. The plaster glows like ... warm cheeks.'

He didn't laugh although she expected he might. Her observations about sculpture were never as lyrical as she would like them to be.

'When Rilke worked as Rodin's secretary he talked about plaster being alive. He thought it had transparent whiteness,' he said.

'I thought Rodin did bronzes.'

'He cast lots of figures in plaster too. Most of them are incomplete, parts of bodies, hands and feet, torsos, legs.'

Transparent whiteness. Yes, she has that. Alix remembered the woman whose husband was not quite dead enough. She looked again at the sculpture and thought, this woman has no heart and yet she is alive.

Alix was half an hour late for dinner on Tuesday night and although Dan did not once mention her lateness, she felt honour-bound to point it out, repetitively. But he waved her apologies away and ordered champagne, poured, lifted his glass and began to toast.

'To ...' he said and she waited for him to finish, to say, 'to us' or 'to you' or 'to art,' or something innocuous and unimportant and not at all memorable. 'To the next six months,' he said.

She raised her glass and asked, 'Why?'

'It's a brain tumour. *Glioblastoma multiforme.*' He knew she'd want the specifics, knew she'd know exactly what *glioblastoma multiforme* meant, not just medically, but to them, to him, to his life. 'The doctor says I've got about six months.'

For some reason, she did not lower her glass. *What* was a brain tumour? And then she remembered. The headaches in the morning. The tripping over nothing when they went for their morning walk. The occasional vomiting. His doctor had wanted him to get it checked out. Probably a virus. And she hadn't gone with him today because she was working and because it was just a virus.

'It shouldn't be summer,' Alix whispered as she took his hand and they both looked out the window at the still-light sky dipping into the harbour. She knew that he was thinking the same as her: that it should have been autumn. They should have been surrounded by trees disrobing themselves, by branches casting their leaves aside to bathe their bark in the last warmth of the season.

CAMILLE

FIVE

Sarah doesn't see me arrive at the café. Jack Darcy does. At least, I assume it is Jack and then he smiles at me so I know that it is.

'I suppose the red hair gave it away,' I say to him as I sit down without shaking his hand.

As I lean across and kiss Sarah's cheek, he says, 'Even without that I'd have known. 'You're just like her.'

And I know that he actually means what he says; he has painted my mother so he knows her bone structure, the tone of her skin, wrinkle patterns, everything, and he would see the differences straight away, if there were any.

Sarah breaks the silence. 'Camille, meet Jack Darcy.'

'I've made some notes,' I say, more to Sarah than to Jack. 'I've listed all the pieces I think we should show and in what order I think they should be exhibited.' I pass a sheet of paper to each of them. Then I hand a document to Sarah, a document I had fussed over and edited until after midnight, trying to decide what to leave in, what to take out. I was ruthless in the end, deleting paragraphs. But I felt as if I was cheating so I restored some of the text, unsure if I was exposing Alix and

Dan or if I was only exposing myself. 'And here's a draft of the beginning of the exhibition notes for the catalogue.'

'Do I get to see those too?' Jack asks.

'Not yet,' I reply.

And Sarah, who knows a little but not too much about Alix and Dan and Jack, but who knows me well enough to sense that I need to speak to Jack alone, takes her coffee and the pile of notes over to another table, saying, 'I'm just going to read through these while you two talk.'

As soon as she leaves, Jack begins to speak. 'I wasn't sure about the whole idea at first. But when Sarah said she'd ask you to curate I thought it might work.'

As he talks I study him, wanting to see the man my mother loved. He is not young any more, probably in his late sixties, but there is no doubting his charisma. I am reminded of George Clooney, old but ageless, greying but the better for it, eyes as clear blue as a child's, smile that is both devilish and enticing. Debonair, I think, which is not a word I have ever used to describe anyone.

I have been silent for too long and he knows I have been appraising, so I say, 'You're better looking than I thought you'd be, now.'

The smile lingers. 'You sound as if you'd be happier if I was an ugly old man.'

'Yes. But I don't know why.' I am honest; my displeasure is not due to loyalty to my father, who was also a tricky combination of the cheeky but dashing artist – perhaps my discontent is due to this similarity. I shrug and respond to his earlier comment about the exhibition. 'It's a romantic idea. I'm sure it will be popular.'

'But not with you.'

I sip my tea and try to raise my voice so that it conveys even a hint of the excitement I had previously felt about curating the exhibition. But it won't come, not here with him. 'That's not true. I like romance as much as anybody.'

'But you think it's a fiction best left to art to depict.'

His blue eyes are studying me now, just as I studied him before. I want to turn away, to squirm, to see what he is seeing: a woman with a frown etched between her eyebrows, jaws strung together, angry at romance.

'Maybe.' I finish my tea. 'Because in real life, romance isn't always enough, is it?'

And he surprises me by agreeing. 'No, it's not,' he says.

And I want to blurt out: but you're the artist. You're meant to defend romance and passion and the impossible. To say that it makes us better people to see the world through art, to imagine that it is not all artifice, that there is something of substance lurking within. Instead I say, 'You weren't enough to keep Alix alive.'

The silence that comes after is not tense, which I thought it might be. It is just full, full of the past, the things that Jack knows and that I don't know.

But then he says, 'She was scared, Camille,' and I stare at him, perplexed. Of all the words I have heard used to describe my mother, scared is not one of them.

Of what? is the obvious question to ask. But that is a bit like asking, *What really happened?* and I'm not sure that I'm ready to find out. Because there's that whisper again, Louisa's whisper: *What will I tell Camille?* and that slippery feeling that what she told me was not the truth.

Jack takes a folded piece of paper out of his pocket. 'After Sarah rang me, I looked through my things to see if I had anything left, from Alix. I found this. Alix never sent it to me. Louisa found it when she was sorting out Alix's stuff. You can use it, if you like, for the catalogue notes.'

When I unfold the paper I can see that it is a letter. I begin to read.

Dear Jack,
I depend upon dead people. In my line of work, someone has to die so that someone else can live. But it was not supposed to be Dan.

You say that you don't know if I love you – I do, you see, but I still love Dan and you will always lose when pitted against him. The fact that you are living renders you unfixable, whereas he has the benefit of being set in the stilled moment of death, a moment at which fantasy gilds memory and he becomes whatever I want him to be: the man whose plaster face I now hold in my hands as once I held his face of flesh and blood and bone.

Here again you cannot compete. The plaster skin defies ageing; he will not frown, he will not rage or cry or scorn. He is luminous in a way you can never be, would never wish to be, because you value the story of the deepening crease around someone's mouth, the varying shades of pigment in a person's skin, the particularity of the blueness of a subject's eyes.

If you knew I had his death mask, what would you say? Would you think of it as sculpture or as the bizarre act of a woman who cannot let go of what is gone? That is not why I keep it; that is not why I cast it.

I love you as much as I can and I keep his face because he will need it when he comes back.

Love,
Alix

'She made a death mask?' is the first question, of the many, that drops from my mouth.

'Apparently. I never saw it. You should ask Louisa about it.' He pauses, then adds, 'If you find it, you should show it in the exhibition.'

'But it's so ... private. She didn't show it to anyone. How can I? Like this letter. It's private too. Why didn't she send it to you?'

'I don't know. Sometimes things become more than they need to be if you keep them secret. I think if you *don't* show the mask, the exhibition will seem like,' he pauses, 'something is missing.'

My phone rings. It's Addie's consultant. I have no choice but to say goodbye to Jack and to Sarah, to step outside, to not give Jack my reply, which was, *I always feel like something is missing.*

I return home long enough to go for a quick run, get changed, read to Rosie and put her to bed. I'm an automaton, but luckily

Julie has taken Rosie to the swimming pool earlier in the day and she is too tired to notice. At 7.00 p.m., Louisa arrives with a parcel of food, homemade pizza this time. 'Hi love.' She kisses my cheek and busies herself with putting the pizza in the freezer and washing the dinner dishes, waving me away when I tell her to leave them, that Paul will do them when he gets home.

'He'll be too tired and so will you. Off you go.'

I pick up my keys, hesitate, and say, 'I met Jack Darcy today. About the exhibition.'

Louisa looks up from the sink and waits, knowing that there is more to come. It is this that I love about her, the quiet patience, the lack of pressure, the absolute trust that I will talk to her. And I always do, I always have.

'It was awkward,' I say. 'We hardly talked about Alix. Well, we did. But not really.'

'Sounds like the kind of first meeting you're bound to have in that situation. See how the next one goes.'

'Louisa?'

'Yes love.'

'You know how you used to tell me stories about Dan and Alix?'

Louisa nods.

'How did you know everything that you told me?'

'When Alix went out at night with Jack, she would drop you off at my house first. She always came a little early and we'd sit out the back, watching you and Fliss on the trampoline and then she'd start to talk. Sometimes she'd talk so much she'd be late for her date. It was as if she'd forgotten where she was, like her mouth was speaking by itself without her mind putting the words there in the first place.'

I shake my head. 'Surgeons aren't impulsive people.'

'Alix was different after Dan died.'

I look at the clock. I've started a conversation that I don't have time to finish but I can't help asking, 'Did Alix make a death mask? Of Dan?'

'Have you looked through those boxes I gave you years ago?'

'Not really.'

'Why not?'

'I don't know. It's like prying. What if I find something that I don't want to find? Once it's found, I can't just shut the lid on the box and pretend it's not there.'

'You don't have any of Dan's things. Imagine if you had none of Alix's either.'

'I have Dan's sculptures.'

'That's not the same as having his possessions. Look in the boxes, love.'

Another question comes tumbling out. 'It's funny that Alix and Dan both died in car accidents. Isn't it?'

'No funnier than Alix falling in love with two artists. Coincidences do happen.'

'So you really think she loved Jack Darcy too?'

'I know she did.'

'You were always so fair to Jack. Didn't it upset you, that maybe she was replacing Dan with Jack?'

'So long as she was happy, it didn't matter. Because if she

was happy, then you would be too. And you were the most important thing.'

I give her a hug, like one Rosie would give me. Then I have no more time left. 'I'd better go. Don't do too much work.'

I leave, knowing that in the half hour it will take for me to get to the hospital and for Paul to come home she will have put on a load of washing, cleaned the kitchen and made my bed.

When I get to PICU, Paul is asleep in the chair, mouth open, face revealing an exhausted sadness that is never there when his eyes are open. I wonder where it goes when he is awake, where he puts it, whether he has also had to turn away or leave rooms today so the tears stay hidden.

Once, I would have found this a tender scene, been touched by discovering something buried deep within my husband. But now as I look at him I wonder if all mothers stop loving their husbands after their children are born, whether any of them admit to having found, in their child, something more enthralling than a love they once thought was their greatest.

'How was your day?'

Paul's eyes snap open, he pats around wildly for his phone and begins scrolling through screens, desperate to regain the hour of lost time that he missed while sleeping. 'Fine,' he mumbles, then he shakes his head. 'Fuck.'

I raise my eyebrows at him and point at Addie.

'She can't hear me,' he says.

'Thanks for pointing that out. Miss something important while you were stuck here?'

He chooses to ignore the sarcasm and replies to my question as if I actually care about the answer. 'I've been waiting for an email all day and of course it came half an hour ago. I can't believe I fell asleep.'

I remember the way he looked in the chair when I came in. Shattered. Splintered into so many small pieces he might never be able to put himself back together again. 'Maybe you're tired,' I say.

It's his turn for sarcasm. He repeats my earlier words. 'Thanks for pointing that out. I'm going to work.'

'I told Louisa you were coming home,' I call to his departing back. 'Ring her.' I pick up my phone and dial home, knowing Paul will forget because he will spend the whole drive from the hospital to work on the phone to people more important than any of us.

I drag a chair over to Addie's bed, lay my head forward onto my folded arms, close my eyes and drift off into an episodic sleep that is always broken by ICU bustle. Then I sense the tiny movement of her eyes opening and I am immediately awake.

'Hi darling.' I smile at her, knowing that smiles are the things she needs to see. I let the fear sit at the back of my throat, hidden behind my epiglottis, where she cannot see it and where it will not make her cry, which would cause everything to unravel.

She doesn't look around, she doesn't ask where she is, she just says, 'Don't go Mummy,' as if the entire time she has been asleep she has known when I have been there and when I have not.

I kiss her cheek. 'I won't go until you can come with me.'

Of course I am lying; mothers lie all the time – if you don't stop pulling your sister's hair you won't be allowed to come to the park, but of course you always end up taking them both to the park because when there are swings and slides and sand there is never any hair-pulling. But this is the answer she wants and so she closes her eyes again; her three-year-old body can do nothing but sleep when it is being attacked from within because of the randomness of her being the *one* child in the statistic, not the fifteen thousand healthy children. I wait a few minutes and then go to find the doctor, breaking my promise to Addie just moments after it has been made.

'She's woken up,' I say to the doctor when I find him, in the middle of his rounds, probably on his way to see us anyway but I know, as a nurse, how to make him see Addie first because, as a mother, I do not care about anyone else.

'We'll get her prepped for the endoscopy in the morning,' he replies. 'Her FBC also suggests hypersplenism so we'll do a CT to check.'

I nod and walk back to Addie's room, realising that we have run out of complications; she has contracted everything and the only thing to do now is suppress them for as long as it takes to find that one perfect, almost triangular, russet-coloured organ.

SIX

I break my promise to Addie once again the next day when she
goes to have her endoscopy because she is sedated and does
not know whether I am there or not and I need, after sitting
with her for fourteen hours, to stretch my legs, to walk, to see
life that does not require intensive care. I ask the nurse to call
me as soon as Addie is out, before she wakes, because she is
always scared, always howling in recovery.

There is a small garden on the north side of the hospital
where everything is miniature, the right size for children:
gnarled bonsai, a fairy grotto inside a stump, a handful of
primary-coloured chairs made for bottoms smaller than my
own. Nobody is there and so I do laps of the path, shivering in
air that is not climate-controlled.

I imagine, as if I am in the room, an endoscope, a tube like
a snake with an eye at each end slithering into my daughter's mouth, down through her oesophagus and into her gut,
sending pictures of swollen and bursting veins though to
the doctor. I will the doctor to stop the bleeding, to fix this
complication for now, to let her bruised body take its chance
to heal.

And it works. They do stop the bleeding. Addie is asleep and stable and worry should loosen its grip. It lets go of Paul; he smiles when the doctor gives us the news.

But of course I have to go ahead and say, 'The cirrhosis will never go away, the hypertension is still there and the varices can come back.'

'She might get a new liver before that happens,' Paul replies.

I don't know why I want him to stop smiling but I do. 'Do you know how many paediatric liver donors there are in a year? Almost none.'

'You said she can have part of an adult's liver.'

I could just nod at this point because what he says is possible. But not likely. 'She's so small. Even the left lobe from an adult liver might not work.'

'Geez Camille, no one could ever accuse you of being optimistic.' And he walks away.

Inside my closed mouth I am shouting, *But all these thoughts are in my head and I don't know how to get them out other than to share them with you.*

Ten years ago, I could not imagine a time when Paul would not wish to know what I was thinking.

We met at a party given by a friend. I saw him as soon as I walked in to the room. He was so tall and his eyes were like the deepest part of the ocean, dark blue and impassable, and I thought of the guys I'd been out with before and how insipid their too-revealing eyes were compared to his. I found a wine and made sure I was always chatting, always laughing, always busy just in case he noticed me. Then we both went to get a drink at the same time and we spoke as we reached for the last bottle of wine.

'I'm Camille,' I said.

'You're beautiful.'

By this time the lights were low and people were dancing so I hooked my finger through the belt loop of his jeans and looked up at him, feeling his groin pressed to mine, our upper bodies separated by a hand space.

'How do you know Sarah?' I asked as I took a sip of the wine.

'I don't. A mate of mine is her cousin. You?'

'We went to uni together.'

'Any more formalities?'

'I think that's it.'

Then we kissed by the bar, not caring about anyone who needed to get past us to find a drink.

But I wanted more so I said, 'Let's go,' and we caught a cab back to my house and soon we were naked on my bed and his hands were on my breasts and he was pushing one of my legs up against my chest so that his tongue could find its way between them and it took only a few minutes before I wanted to come so I pulled him up and rolled him onto his back and then sat astride him, moving fast, so we both came, together, almost as soon as he was inside me.

Like my mother with my father, I moved in with Paul and we became engaged soon after we met. We were gluttonous with each other back then, not just when it came to sex, but also when it came to excavating one another's minds until we felt we knew everything about our pasts, our memories, our dreams and our thoughts. We ignored our friends, our families, the world, because none of those things satisfied us the way our love did.

He was not an artist, for which I was grateful. But I wanted someone with an artistic sensibility and how lucky I was, I thought, to fall in love with a journalist who crafted words and who shared my love for collecting drawings, paintings and sculpture.

We moved into my mother and father's house, which had been left to me and managed by Louisa on my behalf. It was an Art Deco mansion in Elizabeth Bay that had been leased for twenty years to groups of students who had treated it like a hostel. When Paul and I pushed open the high wooden door, we could almost hear, in the wind that made the chandelier crystals whine, the despair it felt at such neglect.

And so for the next couple of years all that mattered was that we got married, were promoted at work and that we fixed the house. I had money, all of my father's money, which Louisa had looked after for me and which I had never spent. Until then, I could not imagine what to spend it on; how could I possibly buy shoes and dresses with money that my father had made from his art?

We camped in the studio while we renovated, with a mattress and sleeping bags for a bed, and a camp stove, saucepan and paper plates for dinner. Nothing tasted like sausage and baked beans when it was eaten on a bed with my legs crossed over Paul's as he showed me the first full-page feature article he'd been asked to write for the newspaper; and as I told him how many lives I'd saved in my first day as a donor coordinator and how much more fulfilling it was than being just a nurse who did a lot of dressing changes and blood pressure checks but very little life-saving; and as both of us planned which gallery we'd visit on the weekend to buy beautiful things to fill our home with, to make it a living piece of art where works were not on show, but part of our life.

The renovations continued around us; Art Deco ceiling roses began to flourish, shining parquetry floors seemed to beckon dancing feet and the fluted entry columns welcomed us each night as we returned home. That is how I remember those years, as a perpetual summer holiday, always anticipating the next room finished, the house finally complete, the moving in, as mindless of noise and dust as campers are of the insects around them.

Then the house was ready and Paul had made me promise to be home by 6.00 p.m. for the great unveiling. I stepped inside just a few minutes late and could see the glow of light from the wall sconces in the living room summoning me through the leadlight doors. On the other side was Paul, in a dinner suit, sitting in one of two leather and chrome Art Deco chairs that we'd been admiring in one of the antique stores in Paddington for some time. He had two glasses of champagne in his hands, along with a white box tied with black ribbon.

'Happy housewarming,' he murmured against my lips as I kissed him.

I opened the present and inside was a long, black silk, bias cut dress with a low back which, when I stepped into the other room to put it on, fitted perfectly. I took my hair down from its ponytail and tipped my head up to free the red waves that had been restrained all day at work.

'Are you ready?' I heard Paul call. 'You know you can get dressed in here.'

'I want to make a dramatic entrance,' I called back, laughing. Then I put on some dark red lipstick that was one of a collection in my handbag and threw open the doors.

Paul smiled. 'Definitely worth waiting for. Shall we dance?'

He held out a hand and I realised he'd found the time to clean up my father's old gramophone and to find an album and put the whole thing together, just for me. So I took his hand and his arms curled around my back as my neck stretched up to meet his and we waltzed together, his fingers stroking the bare skin of my back. We stayed like that for the whole album, lost in our circle, lost in our home, lost in each other.

When the music ended I kissed him, lightly at first, wanting to feel how soft his lips were when they brushed against mine, tasting just the tip of his tongue, feeling the undulation of each rib through his shirt as my hands moved under his jacket and up his back. And then there was no longer any lightness to our kisses; our mouths were pressed hard together and Paul's hands moved inside the curve of my dress to brush the skin of my buttocks and pull me closer to him. Then his hand slid up my back to the line of fabric covering my breasts and his thumbs found my nipples but that wasn't enough so I moved back against the wall while he lifted my skirt and parted my legs and I thrust against him until we were crying out, over and over again.

SEVEN

They have dropped Addie's level of sedation but she sleeps on regardless, her body doing what it needs to do to heal itself. She'll most likely be transferred to a ward tomorrow; it is a sign of progress, albeit temporary.

The ICU nurse sits by her bed, as do I. The nurse is busy, checking monitors, refilling drips, making notes. I have nothing to do; I have read Addie's notes, spoken to the intensivist and the hepatologist and, while I am itching to jump up off the chair so I can help, I know better than to interfere with the nurse's work. I wait for Louisa to arrive and I can't help but overhear a conversation, conducted in an ever louder whisper, at the bedside of the girl nearest Addie.

'She is never seeing him again. I'll lock her in the house or send her away before I let him near her again.' The mother is speaking to a man who is, I presume, the father. The girl has been in a motor vehicle accident and as I listen, it becomes apparent that the girl, who looks about fourteen, has been critically injured in a car driven at speed down the wrong side of the highway by her underage and drunken boyfriend.

The father shrugs and says, 'You'll just end up fighting

with her more if you tell her she can't see him.'

'I'd rather fight with her every minute of every day if it meant she didn't end up here,' the mother replies, clutching her daughter's hand, holding on tight, lest the girl slip away.

Then Louisa arrives and after I give her a hug and pass on some instructions I ask her, 'Did we fight much when I was a teenager? I can't remember ever being grounded or anything like that.'

Louisa laughs. 'Felicity and I fought all the time. But with you, never.'

'I was too busy studying I suppose.'

'You studied a lot. But I do remember one time when you asked if you could go to a party at someone's house and I'd heard that the kid's parents were away and he wasn't supposed to be having a party. I'd just had a huge argument with Felicity about the same thing. So I said no. And you just said okay.'

'I remember that. You told me it was okay to disagree with one another, that I didn't just have to say okay and walk away.'

'That's right.'

I hesitate only a moment and then I say, 'All my friends hated their mothers when I was in high school. I didn't have the luxury. The other girls could hate in the comfort of knowing their mothers would be there regardless. I didn't want to test the fixity of you in my life.'

'I know, love.'

There is a moment of silence and then I hug Louisa again before I go home to search for a death mask.

As soon as I pull out the boxes Louisa gave me so many years earlier, I know the mask is in there. I remember long ago seeing a smaller box inside the larger box; it was heavy and seemed, to someone unwilling to search too far, to have nothing inside other than tissue paper. Of course, beneath the layers, there is the mask.

I take it out and look at it for a while, imagining being so attached to someone that you think they are, beyond all logic, going to come back from death. And I realise that this is how I think of Addie, as being always here, always with me, never gone for more than a matter of hours. It is beyond belief that she could be gone, forever.

There is a noise, suddenly, a shouting, voices raised and I cross to the window to look outside. There are two people on the street with loud voices and at first I think they are drunk and walking back from the pub, that the loudness is possibly joviality but then I realise that it is not. The man is shouting, 'No. I've done everything for you. Everything. I've given it all to you.' And then words I never imagined people might actually say to one another, 'I'll rip your fucking head off.' His voice stretches up higher into the extremities of human emotion, then it breaks and cracks and words are dropped and lost but there is no mistaking his intention. He is striding towards the woman. She is backing away, screaming or pleading. I cannot understand her.

But then a figure appears on the front porch of the house opposite me. A child. A boy of about eight. The woman runs towards him and I realise that these are my neighbours.

A middle-class, suburban family whose children have now heard their father threatening to decapitate their mother. Everything ugly about them, things they have kept so well hidden beneath casual waves and hellos, has spilled out of their house and onto the street in a too-public display of marriage collapse.

Another son appears. His mother shouts something at him. He goes inside. Reappears. The children and their mother jump into a car and drive off. The man walks into the house. The lights are blazing on the empty driveway. They blaze all night. Does he hope they'll return or does he just forget that the lights are on? What do you do when you are alone in your house and your family has just been broken, viciously, before your children's eyes? Do you get drunk? Make telephone calls? The car does not reappear.

When Paul arrives home I want to tell him about it. The lights shine on, across the road, like a warning.

'I'm knackered,' he says, undoing his tie, heading straight for the shower. I wait for him in the kitchen, ready to make coffee, but he does not come down. After half an hour I go upstairs and find him asleep in bed.

As I return to the kitchen I stop and look at a sculpture of my father's that I keep on the sideboard next to the table as if it was something as ordinary as a dinner plate. Because I see it every day alongside my cornflakes, I rarely *see* it; it is like a glass of milk – an essential but unnoticed part of life.

But tonight I notice that the heart the woman is holding in her hand in this sculpture is uneven; it is not the stylised, symmetrical symbol I am used to seeing on greeting cards and romance novels. The woman has taken a piece of the heart into her mouth and I realise, for the first time, that her mouth is puckered slightly, as if the bitten heart had not tasted quite as she thought it would.

NOTES ON AN

EXHIBITION

DEATH MASK

(Plaster, 24 x 18cm. Cast by the artist's wife.)

At least you didn't have to watch him suffer for months on end. That is what people said to Alix when they came to visit her and Dan in the hospital.

Months on end. How Alix had wanted those months on end. She'd known exactly what would happen, the details, the process. Surgery, radiotherapy, chemotherapy. Dan would fight. He wouldn't believe that the treatment could do nothing other than prolong his life, that he could not be cured. The treatment would slow things down, they'd have moments of thinking they'd beaten it, but then there would be no more treatment, just a kind of care labelled as palliative. Drugs for pain, drugs for sleep. Less time out of bed, just an hour or two in a chair by the fire in the studio, her head resting against his knees, his hands tangled in her hair. Then no time out of bed.

About two weeks before, he would no longer recognise her. She would have to get in a nurse to help. Then life would begin to concentrate itself around the heart and the brain. She would watch his body shut off the extremities, watch his legs and arms turn to wet papier-mâché. That would happen about one week before. Then there would be the cessation of movement. Breath. A flatline. No breath.

His life ended just two weeks after their dinner in the restaurant. He became another alive body attached to a brain that had died. The ambos had seen her picture in his wallet and had called ahead to warn someone. He'd tripped, fallen off the curb in front of their house at the exact moment a car came speeding by.

'You'll want to see him,' said Helen, a nurse who was also Alix's friend, taking this as given; Alix had seen so many bodies and their parts, why not this one?

'No,' Alix said.

She turned and walked past broken bodies and found a cab waiting out the front and told the driver that her husband had died so that he'd drive quickly and not say a thing and then she was home and lying on the bed, not wondering where he'd gone, not thinking about why he'd been outside falling off curbs, but staring at a single strand of golden hair sleeping on his pillow and feeling only the cold, hard lack of him.

Of course she returned to the hospital an hour or so later. She talked to him, whispered, *Happy Valentine's Day*, and held his hand even though she knew it was not a rational thing to do. But she had always thought of him as extending from his hands. His hands did not look dead.

In fact, the hand she held looked as it always had, with its palm shaped to fit hers exactly. His fingernails had traces of white beneath them – an accumulation of plaster – his skin was pink and even though his hands were immobile they looked ready to stir, as though at any moment his fingers would reach out for something of flesh or art or substance.

If only she'd kissed him harder and longer that morning. If only she'd rolled over in bed before they got up, wrapped one arm around his waist and then wound her body over his instead of jumping up when the alarm sounded. If only she'd waved to him as she walked down the path to the front gate. If only she'd called him just to say hi. If only she'd taken him out to dinner for Valentine's Day, ordered a bottle of champagne and a plate of oysters, worn the black backless dress that he liked and whisked him off in a plane after dinner to a Fijian island where this could never have happened.

But *if onlys* didn't change anything. So she stopped thinking them. Instead she wrote it all down, everything that she saw and thought and felt as she sat beside Dan's bed; she recorded it all in a diary. Because it was her last chance to hold onto him and she knew, although she did consider it for a moment, that she could not cut off his hands and keep them, so she bore witness to his death in the only way she could.

She watched them carry out the brain-death tests, tests she'd seen a thousand times before, tests that now seemed akin to voodoo. She grimaced as they pressed down hard on his forehead; he slept. She blinked her eyes as they stroked his corneas with cotton wool; he did not. Her pupils shrank when they shone light into his eyes; he continued to stare straight at her. She turned her head away when they poured ice cold water into his ears. They touched the back of his throat and she tasted her lunch in her mouth; he seemed only to smile because of the way they held his mouth. She cleared her throat when they suctioned his bronchi; he did not even cough. When they removed the ventilator she could not help but shout, *Shut up*, at the doctors because their coats rustled loud enough to disguise a gasp that in any case never came. The ventilator was then reattached and time of death, one o'clock, was declared.

It was only then that Alix realised how medicalised her perception of life had become. In order to have a supply of hearts for transplantation, she had to believe in brain death; that doctors like her no longer waited for the heart to die of its own accord. In fact they kept it pumping with a machine; they kept one part of the body alive for days after another part had died. Laws had been passed to accommodate the new definition of death, a definition which facilitated the work she did.

But now she understood, as if for the first time, that this definition assumed that Dan was only Dan within his brain, that he had ceased to be who he was when his brain had died. So who then was she talking to, whose hand was she holding?

She fell asleep in the chair for only ten minutes but the dream she had seemed to go on for all of that time and into the future. She dreamed that she searched Dan's body for death.

She dreamed that she watched them wheel him into surgery to take out his organs. They took out his heart and she wanted it back; it was still beating so there must be a piece of him alive somewhere and all she had to do was find it. She crawled through his blood on the floor of the operating theatre, searching in case it had fallen out and no one had noticed it and then she stood and shouted 'No!' because they were packing his heart in ice and taking it away to give to someone else and she could not let them do it because what if he was in there, in that heart, and she had given him away to another person who would forever after have her husband's soul.

Alix held on to the unsigned consent forms that Helen had given her, forms giving custody of his body parts to a surgeon like her to use to save somebody else's life. The words on each piece of paper were incomprehensible and so she shook her head: once, twice, three times.

Helen misunderstood her confusion and said gently, as if Alix must have forgotten how the system worked, 'Dan had a primary brain tumour, not a secondary one. So he can still be considered for organ donation.'

'I know that,' Alix snapped. She remembered her dream but she could not tell Helen about that, about wanting to keep his heart for herself. Instead she said, 'I can't think of him as a repository. Of his organs as commodities, of his body as a cadaver on a table in an anatomy lab ready to be carved up by queasy medical students, just like I used to saw and cut into cadavers, people who were no longer people, but rather experiments, scientific games.'

'You know his organs aren't commodities,' Helen said. 'They're ...'

'Gifts,' Alix interrupted. 'Yes, I know the theory. But he still looks like Dan. He still is Dan.'

'He's gone, Alix.'

Helen was gentle, kind, just as she should be. And probably right. Because Alix had looked into every part of the human body, beneath every bone, within every muscle and had seen no trace of a spirit, of a soul. She had watched people die in front of her and she had never seen or felt a piece of them projected out of their bodies, into the operating theatre and upwards into the sky.

She put the forms on the floor and said to Helen, 'I always thought it was funny, the way he treated plaster bodies compared to the way doctors treat real bodies. He was so tender; you have to be gentle with plaster. But no one is tender with a body on the operating table.'

'They'll look after him Alix,' Helen replied.

'Not the way I want them to. Even when Dan was using tools for etching or carving, his hands seemed to be whispering to the plaster, coaxing lines to appear on the surface. Lines that opened beneath the soft voice of his fingers.' Alix laughed. 'Listen to me. I sound like an exhibition catalogue.'

Helen shook her head. 'You sound like someone who'll miss her husband.'

'I used to hate the sound of his rasp. Until he told me it was like the tongue of a cat, skimming off the slightest imperfections. When he finished with the rasp, he'd have revealed something new, something that I could never have imagined lay beneath. It was like resuscitation, giving life to what had been just a paste of powder and water.'

Helen did not reply because what could she say to that? So Alix kept talking, saying things that were in her mind, things that she would never have believed, just yesterday, could be in her mind. 'How many times can a person die?'

'What do you mean?' asked Helen, confused at the turn the conversation had taken.

'Just that Dan will die twice if I give his heart away. Because he is dead now, apparently, but he will die again when they remove his heart on the operating table.'

'Alix.' Helen hugged her then because they were friends as well as colleagues and Alix was asking questions that no one, not a friend, not a colleague, not even a priest, could answer.

That was when Alix remembered something she had learned and forgotten, that the Japanese resist the idea of organ transplantation because they understand that to remove a part of the body leaves a person's spirit trapped between life and death. That is where Dan is now, Alix thought, and she didn't know which was the better choice to make: to consign him to an absolute death or to have him always in this liminal space where she could not quite let go, nor could she quite hold on.

After Helen left, Alix picked up the consent forms. If she signed them, said yes, then the anaesthetist would administer a muscle relaxant and then a cut would be made along the midline of his abdomen. Alix ran her finger down the line the surgeons would make and rested her hand on his stomach as she imagined his abdomen excavated, then his sternum opened, the heart and lungs paralysed, the blood from his heart clamped and stopped, the ventilator shut down, the heart and lungs removed, his now-cold heart afloat in a bag, prostheses inserted to replace his missing eyeballs and then his body stitched, and washed and dressed. Evisceration as opposed to resuscitation.

She woke later from another sleep in the chair by the bed needing to find something that she read in a book Dan gave to her. The book was by Rilke, about Rodin's plaster sculptures, and Dan gave it to her when he was trying to explain why he used plaster as a medium, rather than a passing phase between clay and bronze.

She knew the drive home would take only five minutes so she got in the car and sped, going too fast down suburban streets, running lights that were no longer orange but a distinctly bloodish shade of red.

In Dan's studio it didn't take her long to find the book. It took her longer to find the quote, so she sat in Dan's chair behind his desk and scanned through pages until there it was. 'A hand laid on the shoulder or limb of another body is no longer part of the body to which it properly belongs: something new has been formed from it and the object it touches or holds, something ... which is nameless and belongs to no one.'

What good did that do, she thought. *If I give Dan's heart away, does he then become nameless, does he then belong to no one?*

She put the book down, closed her eyes and tried to see him. To defy Rilke by owning Dan with her mind's eye. She began with his face. Dan's face. No one else's. An arrangement of bones, nose, teeth and muscle that made him recognisable as him, that made him the person he was.

As she thought this, she understood for the first time the impulse for art. That it was her turn to sculpt. He was the subject now. Not her.

She'd watched Dan cast enough plaster to know that speed was required: not the desperate rush of surgery to fix a massive embolism but the calibrated haste of a transplant. She told the nurses that she did not want to be disturbed and knew they would obey her because she was a doctor. Then she closed the door to his room and stood beside his bed, seeing, for instance, the true colour of his eyelashes; they were blonde at the roots and dark honey at the tips. A detail the wax would not capture. A detail only her mind could preserve and she had almost missed it even though she'd seen those eyelashes almost every day for two years.

She spread a sheet over the floor, took a bucket and poured in some water, filtering plaster dust through her fingers until it floated in small mounds on the surface. Then she placed her hands in the bucket and stirred. She tore up another sheet into strips, dipped the strips into the plaster and wound them over his face. She scooped up fistfuls of plaster and smoothed it over the fabric, making sure the eyelashes were coated, the lines on his face filled in and the nostrils opened. His lips were stretched and bruised by the ventilator, a detail she did not want to keep so she reshaped the plaster to copy his mouth the way she remembered it.

She sat and waited while the mask set, watching it cool and harden, watching it trap his face in a way that memory could not, watching it claw back what little she could keep of him. Then she cut grooves into the plaster, moistened it a little and carved out the curls of his hair, the fineness of his eyebrows and the shape of his pupils as they would be if his eyes were open. It was time to sit and wait again, to watch the plaster solidify and the drops of water weep over this new layer of skin as the air drew the tears he could not shed from the plaster shell.

Alix did one more thing, in a toilet cubicle near ICU, before he was taken away. She used the pregnancy test kit that had sat unopened in her bag since the day of Dan's accident. Then she went to his bedside to tell him.

'We did it this time,' she said. She took his hand and placed it on her stomach wondering which force was the strongest: the instinct of the baby to live and grow or the instinct of her husband to die and disappear. She felt a pressure, like magnetic opposites repelling, and concluded that both forces were even.

CAMILLE

EIGHT

I am looking after a DCD case, a donation after cardiac death. The patient has suffered an unsurvivable brain injury but she isn't brain-dead. The intensivist has made the decision that if we withdraw cardio-respiratory support, her heart will stop within a short time. The family have agreed to this. They have also agreed to donate all the organs that they can after she dies.

She needs to die within sixty minutes or her organs will suffer too much damage and be useless. Only if she dies within thirty minutes can we use her liver. We have explained to the family that they will have five minutes with her after time of death is declared, then they must stand down. If they cannot, donation will not go ahead.

Everyone is tense. The tiniest thing can destroy the uneasy equilibrium that exists at this time between us and the patient's family. We have to respect the patient as they die. We have to respect the family as they sit and watch. Lastly, we have to respect the organs that will help someone else live. The needs of the family and the needs of the organs are really incompatible. The organs require haste. A speedy death. A speedy retrieval. The family need time.

We move the patient to the operating theatre which has been set up for the retrieval surgery. The family cry and wait. I continue ECG and blood pressure monitoring so I know when the irreversible cessation of circulation occurs. I continue to administer analgesia for pain.

Thirty minutes passes. She is still alive. We have lost a liver. I call the retrieval team and the transplant team and the patient who'd been prepped for a new liver receives the news. *The liver was incompatible,* is what he'll be told and he'll know that this could mean anything from the family changing their mind at the last minute to the liver being damaged in some way. Forty-five minutes. ECG shows continuing circulation. Fifty minutes. No change. After one hour she is still not dead. The lungs, kidneys and pancreas are now *incompatible.* We lose our last remaining hope.

We take the patient back to ICU. I talk to the family, offer my support but they do not want anything from me. They would prefer not to donate tissue now. They have had enough.

I prepare to leave. The patient is not going to be an organ donor so she is not my case any more. Another nurse takes over.

'Sorry,' the family say.

You didn't tell us she was such a stubborn old bitch, is what I don't say.

I am home in time to read Rosie a book before her afternoon sleep. She chooses *Addie and the Bad Fairy.* We read it three times until I close it and say, 'Time for bed.' I have a pile of bills to pay, laundry to fold, dozens of emails from friends that I need to reply to, not to mention an exhibition to curate, and the sooner I get Rosie into bed, the sooner I can begin. 'Let's put your sleeping bag on.'

'Fairy one,' Rosie says.

'The fairy bag is dirty. You spilt milk on it last night. What about the one with pussy cats on it?'

'Fairy one,' Rosie repeats, as if I have not even spoken.

I walk to her room and return with a sleeping bag covered in frolicking kittens. 'This one is especially cuddly.' I reach out for her but she runs away and stands on the other side of the room, watching, waiting.

'I'm not chasing you today. Time for bed.' I wait with the bag on my lap but she does not move so I walk over to her.

She runs off, giggling.

'Rosie! No. Time for bed.'

She stops running and waits. I know that if I move towards her, she will run away again.

'Okay.' I put the bag down on the ground. 'Mummy will have to go if you can't come here and put your bag on. I'm going to count to five. One, two ...' I make it to five and she stays where she is, grinning.

'Off I go then.' I walk towards the door. She doesn't relent. I open the door. Nothing. I step outside and close it. It is only when I begin to walk up the path that I hear her cry out and run towards the door. I wonder what I am going to do if she ever realises that I have no intention of going anywhere, when this trick stops working.

I walk back inside, squat on the floor with the bag and put her on my lap. She arches back and pushes away from me. I hold her, firmly, pushing her arms through the holes. Her legs kick and I struggle to hold her down and connect the zip.

'No, Mummy, no,' she cries, kicking and pushing and arching.

I get one leg in the sleeping bag but she jerks it straight out as I reach for the other. She thrusts her head up and knocks my teeth into my lip. 'Ouch!' I shout and as my hand moves instinctively to my mouth Rosie pulls her arm out of the armhole. I scrabble for her limbs. The zip breaks. I shove her off my lap and onto the floor.

'Happy now?' I yell. 'You've broken it. What a waste of money.' As if she has any idea what I mean. What is it, to an eighteen month old, to waste money? She doesn't even know what money is for. But I can't stop. 'You're a naughty girl. I should put you to bed in just your pyjamas. If you don't care about being cold, neither do I.'

My voice gets louder and louder. I am standing over a baby who is sitting on the floor in a broken sleeping bag, crying, 'Mummy fix,' as she points at the zip.

'Mummy can't fix. If you'd just lie still while I put on your bag it wouldn't have broken. I don't know why you have to make something so simple be so hard.' I am tall and loud and mean. She is tiny and sad and my daughter. I want to smack her. I pick her up instead. Sing 'Hush Little Baby' over and over. Imagine all the other things I could be doing. Having a cup of tea. A bath. Going for a run, feet hitting the pavement, moving fast and far away.

'Do you pray for a drowning? Or for a mother to take her eyes from the road long enough to smile at her child and swerve to the wrong side of the road?'

'Of course not.'

Paul and I are lying in our bed, backs facing one another and separated by a space that could accommodate at least another person.

'I do,' I say.

Paul rolls onto his back and stares at the ceiling. I wonder what he sees. The geometric plaster patterns of the deco ceiling rose, perhaps. In a certain light, it looks as though each of the arrowhead sides is pulling away from the centre, straining to separate from the unity of image they create. Tonight, though, the rose looks at rest; it is simply a piece of decorative art, inert, coming to life only in the imagination of its viewer.

As my eyes adjust to the dark, I realise that Paul's gaze is lowered; he sees neither inertia nor activity in the rose but simply the shape of his own thumbs, pads pressed together, betraying a tension that his fingers, which rest on his chest, are better at hiding.

He says, 'We don't *want* another child to die just so Addie gets a liver. For some other parents to have to bury their child instead of us.'

'Of course we do. You just don't like to say it.'

'Is that such a bad thing?'

'Yes. If we don't want it enough we might not get it.'

'Wanting it and saying it are two different things.'

'And pretending not to think it is better? Lets you sleep at night?'

'Yes.'

He is so fucking placid, lying there in the bed with his morals, that all I want is to provoke him, to make him yell, so it's not just me shouting at someone who looks as though he is already defeated. I say, 'Tonight I pray to God for a kid to fall off the monkey bars and hit their head hard, really hard, on the concrete.'

Paul stands up, throws on his robe and says, 'I'm going to watch TV.'

He is gone before I can accuse him of preferring the safety of an American sitcom to the reality of children dying.

My thoughts prod me like the pea beneath the princess's mattress. I get out of bed and creep down to the studio, hearing the low murmur of the TV as I pass Paul but he does not hear me.

Inside the studio, I walk over to a sculpture, the size of a doll, that sits alone on a stand. It is one of my favourites and it is not one of my father's; it is a bronze of a pregnant woman but it is not softly curved and expectant. Instead the woman has a hand on one hip and she is leaning slightly to the left. The muscles of her legs show the strain of back pain and the impossible quest to find a comfortable position in which to stand. Her belly button is protruding and it looks as if something secret and private has suddenly been thrust into full view. The usually hidden and tucked away parts of the navel are precisely carved and strike the viewer as real, even though the viewer could not possible know – whoever sees the interior spaces of their navel?

The woman's ankles are full of fluid and the bronze appears soft and spongy, as if you could reach out and lose your fingers in the flesh, searching for bones that are not normally so well covered. Her face shows the loss of sleep that she will never regain and the fatigue of carrying the globe of her belly everywhere, of never being able to take it off and put it away, of having to put up with the wriggling, kicking creature inside, of bearing the tightness of yet another practice contraction. Her eyes hold the knowledge that, even after the baby is born, her body will still carry an impression of pregnancy; in the small haemorrhoid that will reappear whenever she decides to eat more bread and less fruit; in the ridge of hardened skin along her perineum that will be left even after the tear has healed; and in her belly button, which will forever after be a wider hole, stretched open like a mouth ready to scream.

The door to the studio opens and Paul steps in. He is wearing a T-shirt that used to be blue and is now bleached white, and soft with age and wear. I look at this T-shirt and wonder why we have not aged into softness like that shirt.

He walks over to the desk and half-sits, half-leans against it. He is silent but it is not a closed silence; it is a listening silence. I put the sculpture back in its place and the bronze touching the wood sends a low tone into the room. It is into this harmony of silence and resonance that I speak.

'They're not real.' I stop, listen to the sound of the bronze woman fade out and then continue. 'The donors. The bodies I see everyday. They're like sculptures in a way, detached from life. But they're not at all sensual; you don't want to touch them the way you do this woman.' I gesture to the piece I have just returned to its stand. 'The ones at the hospital are these awful intellectual works, works without emotion, because nothing, not imagination or belief or looking upon them can change anything about them. That's why I can wish for another one. Because they aren't real.'

The silence continues after I finish; it is now reflective and I let it extend as Paul's thoughts wrap around my words. He looks directly at me and I see that his eyes are still the same as they were when we met, depthless, impassable, and that I know how to dive through to the bottom, into the wreck, and that perhaps we are going there now.

'You couldn't do your job if they were real,' he says.

I nod.

'Why don't you stop, just for now, until Addie's better? You can't spend every day lost within death.'

Lost within death. I had forgotten my husband's eloquence, his ability to translate, to understand. I put out my hand and he takes it and pulls me closer, tucking my head onto his chest which is where I say, 'I can't stop. Because there has to be someone like me in a hospital somewhere when Addie's liver comes in.'

And then the tears spill, into the years and the fineness of Paul's shirt. I can feel his tears falling too, over my hair and down my cheek, tears that polish our skin like a plaster so brilliant I can see both of our faces reflected there, together.

NINE

I go back up to bed with Paul and lie down beside him. His hand reaches for mine and so do his lips. At first it feels like kissing a stranger; it feels like something I am too old to be doing, like a skill I have forgotten to practise. I can't remember the last time we kissed with open mouths, not just a scrape of lip on cheek as we say goodbye in the mornings. I am almost shy of my body and of his, uncertain where to put my hands, unsure what it is that he likes.

The sex we have is neither erotic nor especially arousing; it is two people trying to remember the other, trying to discover the body of the person they married, trying to find out if there is anything left beneath the arguments and the worry and the fear.

Paul falls asleep soon after we finish, lying flat on his back like he always does after sex. That, at least, has not changed.

I haven't dreamed about Paul since Addie has been in the hospital. I wonder where those dreams have gone; I cannot remember what it was like to wake in the morning feeling that love which, even though it vanished quickly, was better than feeling the way I do now.

I will my husband to come into my night thoughts but he stays away, tucked under the doona on his side of the bed, warm, asleep, breathing lightly. I reach out a hand to him, at around three in the morning when I have been awake for more than an hour. I stroke the skin along his hip, lightly because I do not want to wake him; his skin shivers so I move my hand away. I pick up my mother's diary, go downstairs, turn on the light and curl up on the sofa with cognac and chocolates, as if I am sitting down with the latest bestseller. But I can't bring myself to open the covers.

I wait until it is five in the morning and the light is about to creep over the sky. I put on my running gear and take off, fast, too fast, so I am nearly out of breath before I have even reached the park. But something takes over, a reflex that keeps my feet thumping into the ground, my lungs opening and contracting, my body moving forward.

I am sweaty and panting when I return to the house almost two hours later. As I stretch by the front door, I watch the man from across the road fill his car with possessions: a laundry basket full of clothes, a pile of books not in a box, a surfboard. He trips in and out, stuffing the car like a Christmas turkey.

How easy he makes it seem to break up a marriage. It is simply moving things from one location to another, I think as he drives away. A bit like organ transplantation. A heart in one body and then a relocation as it finds another chest to beat within. A chair in one house and then a relocation as it finds another living room to sit within.

My phone rings and it is Sarah, wanting me to come down to the gallery, to show me something. 'I'll stop by on my way to the hospital,' I say as I run inside to shower, hug Rosie, tell Paul that he'll have to be the one to wait for Julie, and then leave again.

'Close your eyes,' instructs Sarah as I step inside the gallery.

'Why?' I ask, shaking my head at the thought that there could be anything surprising for her to want to show me.

'Go on, Camille, just humour me.'

'Okay.' I cover my eyes with my hand for extra effect and let her lead me forward.

We stop and then she says, 'You can open them now.'

'Oh,' I say and I reach out my hand, touch one of the sketches on the wall in front of me, feel the shallow groove the pen has left when transferring ink to the paper.

'I think these should go in the exhibition too.'

'I thought I was the curator.'

'You are, but you'd never dream of including these.'

'I haven't seen them for such a long time. How did you get hold of them?'

'I rang Paul and told him what I was after. He left a key out for me and told me to hunt through the studio one day when you were at the hospital. I knew you'd have kept them. You'd never throw art out.'

I give Sarah a half-smile, the curling upwards of one side of my mouth. 'Yes, but are they art?'

'Of course they are.'

They are a series of pen and ink sketches that I drew at university. Each sketch is of a part of the body, a subscapularis, a lung, a humerus. They are precisely drawn, except that they are not. In each, I have changed a detail, something small and almost unworthy of notice. The humeral head is, for instance, not shaped like a crescent moon but is scalloped – a lace edge to decorate the scapula. The arteries of the lungs do not reach out like fingers; instead they turn back in on themselves like the heads of birds at rest.

'Precise but restrained.' I quote our tutor's feedback but she has heard it before and shakes her head.

'What's he ever produced that anyone can remember? Nothing.'

'Nor have I.'

'Only because you stopped, Camille. I always thought you were mad, doing nursing and art history. I mean, no one does that. Then, when you showed me these, I understood. You could get right inside a body, inside what it means to be alive, in a way no one else could.'

I laugh. 'If only I could still get right inside what it means to be human. My life would be a whole lot simpler.'

'I always thought of them as what would be inside Dan's sculptures, if you could turn them inside out.'

'Yes,' I whisper, in the same way I used to imagine my father whispering to me as I drew, my only connection to him an unreal voice describing not what to draw, but what lay beyond that, the soul of the piece. In those moments I knew that we humans had it wrong; we did not have a soul or a spirit – we found it only within art.

After I leave Sarah, I sit with Addie, who is in a ward, not ICU, and I have never been so happy to see a hospital ward. Because a ward means progress, improvement. I hear from the nurse about a child a couple of years older than Addie who has just had a successful liver transplant. Everyone is happy. We all like stories such as these where children receive livers, where their bodies accept the livers, where there is a Good Outcome.

I think, *That could be us*. We might just play the waiting game and win. Addie might be the most compatible child when the next liver comes in. She might stay healthy enough while we wait. She might even be able to wait at home. So my face is full of a smile when I see her.

'Mummy!' she cries and we hug squeezily, squashily. Her face is full of a smile too.

I open my bag and peep inside. 'Hmmm, I wonder if there's anything in here for a little girl. How about this?' I pull out my sunglass case and she giggles and shakes her head.

'No?' I say. 'Hmmm, what else is there?' I rummage around and this time I produce my credit card.

'No, Mummy,' she laughs, wincing just a little because something must hurt when she laughs and I suddenly think, even though it is only a game we are playing, how unfair it is of me to make her wait for what I have in my bag when she is about to face the most crucial wait of her life.

'Sorry darling,' I say and I give her a kiss and pull a sticker book out of my bag and plump up her pillows to hold her weight better. Then I sit beside her on the bed and help her peel away the stickers and put them in the right place in the book. But soon, even something that simple tires her out and she yawns so I hop off the bed, lay her pillow down flat, tuck her under the sheet and watch her fall straight into a heavy sleep.

I sit down on a chair and begin to sort through the pile of mail in my handbag. I push the window-faced envelopes aside and pull out a thick, creamy envelope that is addressed in writing I do not recognise. I open the envelope and a photograph falls out, as well as a handwritten letter. The letter is from Jack. *I found a photograph that I thought you'd like*, it says. *It was the happiest Christmas of my life.*

Great, I think. Jack has succumbed to the curse of the elderly and is spending all his spare time sorting through mementoes from the past and now I've been made the beneficiary. Then I look at the photograph and realise it is no ordinary keepsake.

It is of a Christmas Day – there is a tree in the background and a pile of presents, half-opened. At the bottom of the tree sit three people. Alix. Jack. Me. I am sitting on Alix's lap and I am grinning up at Jack. He is smiling at me and holding Alix's hand tightly in his own. We look like a family.

I calculate quickly. I must be two years old. Soon, there will be no more Alix and, as far as I am aware, I will never see Jack again, until a meeting I organise with him to discuss an exhibition. How far grief ripples, I think. To people I'd never even considered. Like Jack.

I look down at Addie and realise that ripple is not the

right word. If she doesn't get a liver in time, if she were to ... well, it wouldn't be a ripple of grief that I felt but a riptide and I wonder if you can ever escape such a thing completely. Perhaps we are already in it, Paul and I, dipping our feet into its roiling edges every time we put Addie in an ambulance, every time we hunch beside her bed in ICU.

Paul comes in after lunch so I can spend the afternoon with Rosie at the park, and instead of firing a list of instructions at him I ask, 'How are you?'

He is scrolling through something on his phone and he doesn't look up as he says, 'I'm in the middle of editing a piece.' He sits down in the chair I have vacated and begins to tap the phone, shaking his head.

'Don't forget to give Addie a kiss,' I say.

'She's asleep. I don't want to wake her up.'

Because then you wouldn't have time to finish your piece. I swallow the words because he is here and that's what matters and it's not his fault that he has work to do.

It is mothers' group day at the park; I haven't been for a few weeks and the children look older and the mothers more tired than the last time we met.

Everyone puts on their sympathetic faces as Rosie and I approach.

One of the mothers says, 'Good to see you. We're all praying for you.'

Another chimes in with, 'I'm sure Addie'll be home soon.'

'You're due for some good luck.' They all nod and smile, thinking, *Thank God it's not my child.*

Why do women always seek to press trouble out of their lives with chirpy platitudes, like hands moulding bubbles out of clay? Why can't someone ask how Addie is and listen, really listen, so they come part way to understanding what I might say in response.

Fuck positive thinking. I look up at the sky and remember how often in art it is portrayed as an image of the divine. 'If all I have to rely on is luck then I'm ...' I am about to say *fucked* but stop because of the children. I imagine *putti*, fat and rapturous baby angels hopping from cloud to cloud in the sky above, the tiny leftover souls of children who ran out of luck. 'I'm hoping to be very lucky.' I finish my sentence in the expected way because it is not their fault that they have no idea, not their fault that they don't want to talk to me about my dying child. Because to talk about it is to think about the possibility of their child dying too.

Rosie runs towards the playground calling out, 'Swings!'

I peel away from the group who have, in any case, come to the end of the stock phrases that they think can serve them in such a situation and who are now shifting their feet in the silence, eyes turned towards their children, searching for distractions.

'Careful,' I hear one of the mothers shout to her child who is climbing a ladder up to the slide. 'You don't want to fall.'

Be quiet, I want to shout at the mother. Because to have the chance to fall from the slide is better than never having had the chance to climb. 'That's what bandaids are for,' I mutter as I walk towards Rosie.

I push Rosie's swing five hundred times, back and forth, but she wants more, more. The sensation of flying, of fresh air, of being with her mother at the park, is something she is afraid will vanish if I stop.

Eventually she says, 'Turtles.'

We take the plastic bag of dehydrated fish around to the lake, away from the group of mothers and children spread over the grass, and throw handfuls into the water. Rosie squats by the edge and I keep a hand tucked around her waist in case she leans too far forward and topples in.

'More,' she shouts every time her hand empties of smelly, bony fish.

'There's a big one.' I point to a turtle that is poking its eyes above the water in search of food. Rosie throws a fish to him.

'And there's a little baby,' I say as a much smaller turtle swims cautiously forward.

I try to help her aim her arm so the fish lands near the baby but of course it doesn't and she feeds the bigger turtle instead.

'Mama.' Rosie points to a turtle swimming near the baby. 'Dada,' she says, pointing to the larger one.

'Is that bubba, mama and dada turtle, do you think?'

Rosie nods. Every book we read at the moment, every picture we look at needs to have a bubba, a mama and a dada according to Rosie. She assigns these roles to pictures even when it is quite clear that it is simply a picture of people or animals who hold none of these roles.

'Addie,' she says when another turtle swims up to her invented family group. 'Slow.'

Then she stands and runs off; she has seen a duck and wants to chase it. Her little legs waddle, moving not too fast because they are short and uncoordinated but she must think she is soaring over the grass because she has her arms outstretched and she is giggling. I take off after her and she squeals. She is being a child, being everything she cannot be when Addie is around because Addie is sick and slow.

I stop to catch my breath because a thought has snatched it away; the thought of what has been taken from her, my Rosie, just because her sister was born with a one-in-fifteen-thousand disease that I have fooled myself into thinking of as a sea dragon lurking beneath the ocean of our lives.

NOTES ON AN

EXHIBITION

WHAT SHE HAS LEFT OF HIM

(Plaster, 32 x 32cm, incomplete. Named by the artist's wife for the first retrospective of his work after his death.)

Never. So many promises have that word in them. I'll never leave you, I'll never stop loving you, I'll never forget you. Promises or lies? No, things that should never be said – there's that word again – because someone will always leave and then the loving stops and forgetting begins. That was what Alix was most afraid of.

The day after Dan died Alix went to the electrical store down the road and bought a single bed electric blanket. She took it home and put it on his side of their queen bed. Then she turned it on and waited until that piece of the bed was layered with an almost human warmth, a warmth that she used to curl into at night when her feet were cold and Dan's were not. She lay for an hour or so beside the hot blanket but then got up, switched it off and tore it from the bed. The warmth it cast was not bodily; she could not feel the slight prickle of his leg hair or the weight of him indenting the bed. There was just air and seared sheets and a plaster mask on a pillow which, when she saw it lying there in a place meant for him, became not even a likeness, just an amateur art project, a bit like the foetus growing in her belly.

What she has left of him: clouds of pubic hair caught in the fluff on the bathroom floor, oiled finger and lip prints pressed onto his unwashed wine glass, a stack of coins on the kitchen bench, a five o'clock shadow in the basin, dead skin on the soap, Hunter S. Thompson's *Fear and Loathing in Las Vegas* open on his bedside table, dirty shirts in the washing basket, a used tissue in the bin.

Or at least she would have had those things if her mother had not organised a cleaner to come while they were out at the funeral to take away everything that Alix had left of him.

Dan's wake was in the garden by his studio. Alix would never have found out what her mother had done until after everybody had gone except that she had a headache caused by the constant pressure of her mother's hand on her left shoulder and so she went into the house to get the Panadol.

She noticed the smell first. It was like Domestos, like the hospital. Scoured. Then his last dirty plate. Gone from the sink. The pile of newspapers she bought to read to him. Gone from the coffee table. No washing in the laundry. No towel in the bathroom. She thought at first of thieves. But then she noticed his scent – of chalky plaster, ginger tea and the cinnamon of his aftershave – had been sucked from the air and she knew the thief was her mother.

'Alix.' The pressure of that hand on her shoulder again. 'It had to be done.'

Alix was only aware of the fact that her clenching jaw was making her headache worse, the pain wrapping itself like a swathe of bandages from one side of her head to the other. She was about to speak, to shout, *How dare you*, but the smell of disinfectant, the smell of her work lodged in her home was causing the Vegemite toast she'd had for breakfast to rise to her throat and into her mouth and then she was staring at semi-digested bread splattering onto the floor. Her jaw released and her head loosened. If he had nothing to read – no open book – if he had nothing to dry himself with – no towel waiting – then how could he ever return? She said to her mother, 'Please leave.'

'I'll get someone to clean this up,' her mother replied, pointing, but not looking, at the floor.

'Someone? Get the same cleaners back to finish the job? Can't bend down with a mop and do it yourself?'

Alix knew she was using her height advantage, knew she was leaning forward and towering over her mother's head, and she did this until her mother turned, stepped over the vomit and walked towards the front door.

Then Alix remembered. 'No,' she shouted and ran out of the house, through the garden and into the studio. On a table in the middle of the room was the beginning of a round belly, the navel only lightly shaped in, the tautness of the skin apparent as it reached around and over the bundle inside.

'Thank God,' Alix whispered as she picked it up, curled in a chair and rested the sculpture against her own not-yet rounded belly. That piece was the last one, The End, incomplete, just like Dan.

In the garden, the guests could hear Alix sobbing like a hungry baby, inconsolable because the only thing that could sate her had been buried in the ground that day.

Alix never spoke to her mother again.

Every morning after Dan was gone, every morning of her pregnancy, Alix woke at 5.30 a.m. and ran along the harbour. She did this again after her shift had finished at work.

Louisa told her that she needed to rest, to save some energy for the baby. Louisa even said to Alix, 'You don't want anything to happen to the baby, do you?'

'I don't know,' Alix replied.

So Louisa didn't ask her about it again because she hoped that if Alix didn't think about it, then *I don't know* would not become *yes*. That Alix would remember the baby was what she had left of Dan.

And running occupied Alix's mind with thoughts other than the baby. As she ran she concentrated on the composition of her footsteps over the familiar path. Days of high tides were full of puddles and mud, so she had to turn around and go back when pounding through the water in the cold was more than her feet could bear. Low-tide summer mornings were strewn with beer cans, food wrappers, cigarette butts and trodden grass. Summer afternoons were families and lovers eating ice-creams, ferries and boats passing by on the water. Weekend evenings were carefree, drinks all round, backless dresses, a bite to eat, and sunlight till late so it always felt early and no one ever seemed tired. Winter afternoons were as cold as death, the path bare of lovers and families, no boats, no ferries, only the drip of tears falling and her shoes squeaking in mud and leaf and soil.

AUSCULTATION

(Plaster, 40 x 44cm. One of very few works by the artist that includes elements other than the human body.)

The first week after Dan died was a series of telephone calls.

Telephone call number one: would Alix be the guest of honour at a retrospective of Dan's work next year?

No. It was not that she had anything against the looking backwards to the past implied by the word retrospective. It was the implication that there could be some kind of survey or representation of his life's work. That Dan was complete, finished. Which of course he was not.

Telephone call number two: would she come to dinner at Louisa's that night?

No. To go to dinner by one's self was to admit that she was by herself. Whereas opening the fridge seven times before she went to bed and removing an apple or a piece of cheese or a tub of yogurt and eating them while walking around the house was something she often did if he was away or out or working late.

Telephone call number three: Louisa again. Was there anything she needed?

No. How else to answer a question to which the answers were infinite? Was there anything she needed? There were a great many things that she needed but the real question was: how was it possible to open the plaque at the cemetery and take out what she needed when she knew *he* was not there, merely his leftovers.

Telephone call number four: would she fill in at work tonight for Ian who'd had to go home?

Yes. Because then the phone calls would stop.

When she arrived at work she completed her rounds quickly and competently; she might be grieving but others were dying. Her stethoscope was her constant companion, a little like her big toe in that it was always attached to her but she didn't notice its presence. She used it thoughtlessly, not the way one uses an index finger, with pointed intent, but without thinking, caught in that unconscious space between sleeping and alertness that is so easy to fall into on a long drive.

It was not an expensive stethoscope and she'd had it since university. But its beauty lay in its ability to deliver auscultation. She'd told Dan about auscultation back when they used to sneak into the anatomy lab at night and he'd made a sculpture around that time of a stethoscope pressed against a heart in an open chest. He'd been struck by how the folded-back skin of a chest looked like the pages of a book and so the chest had been sculpted to look like a book and Alix had always thought the stethoscope had the appearance of an eye.

At first this made her frown, because a stethoscope was like a third ear; it didn't *transmit* the sounds that beat below the skin, it heard them: lubdub, lubdub if listening to the heart;

he-haaa if listening to the lungs; and sssssss if listening to the stomach. But then, she thought, auscultation was dialogue, so it could be read. As in a novel, it had exposition: the lubs, the haas, the ssss. It had subtext. That was the thing she was listening for, the slightest nuance in the rhythms, the merest disturbance in the expected patterns of those hidden sounds of the body.

If she could not have Dan's conversation, then auscultation was the only other talk she could tolerate.

'Matthew's biopsy shows moderate rejection.'

Alix sighed, not because of what the cardiologist had said but because she had to take her stethoscope out of her ears. She calculated quickly. 'He's a week post-transplant isn't he?'

The cardiologist nodded.

'Have you spoken to him yet?'

'I thought he'd want to hear it from you.'

Alix paused for only a moment. A moment long enough to savour the victory. That the cardiologist had not simply bypassed her and gone straight to the patient. That he must, at last, be thinking of her as a heart transplant surgeon. Asexual. Not a woman any more.

So she and the cardiologist went to the ICU together to tell the patient. The first sound they heard was Matthew's monitors screaming. He was in cardiac arrest. Adrenalin, the defibrillator, compressions; these tools had all been used, Alix could see, but none had worked. So Alix jumped on the bed, straddled Matthew and took over compressions, shouting,

'Let's get him to the OR. We'll open him up, massage his heart and work out what needs fixing.'

A nurse unlocked the bed brake, another threw the IV bags, defibrillator and portable monitors onto the bed and the cardiologist pumped the ambu-bag as they began to move.

'Get the fuck away from that patient, Nurse.' The intensivist had arrived and was referring to Alix.

She didn't bother to answer because saving a man from dying was more important than wheeling out the oft-repeated line, *I'm a doctor*.

The cardiologist did it for her. 'That's Dr ...'

But he didn't finish. Because the intensivist, who knew exactly who Alix was, had sidled up next to Alix and was whispering in her ear, just loud enough for Alix and the cardiologist to hear, 'You can straddle me like that later, when I fuck you.'

Alix didn't listen. Instead she was glad that, unlike in Dan's sculpture, hearts could not be read, that no one could flip open her chest and read the things printed inside. She remembered her first day as a surgical intern when she, the only female, was selected to stick her hand into another man's chest and perform open heart massage while the other interns took bets on how long it would be before she puked or passed out. Later, she discovered that the female change rooms servicing the operating theatres were labelled Nurses, whereas the male change rooms were labelled Doctors. She'd lost count of the number of times a patient asked her to leave and send in *a real doctor*. But the thing that made her change her name, become

Alix instead of Alixandra, was when a surgeon brushed his hand along the side of her breast every time he asked her to step in closer so he could teach her. Consultants who didn't know her might look at a list and call for a Dr Alix, but no consultant ever called for Dr Alixandra if they could help it – certainly not if all they required was assistance with a patient.

She had stopped noticing the taunts when she met Dan because being in love was more powerful than harassment, insult and abuse. Now it was time to become someone else all over again.

After she had finished assisting in an operation that should have been hers to run with, Alix ordered a repeat biopsy on Matthew. She went with the cardiologist while he conducted the biopsy and watched as he put a cannula through the jugular vein and took out a piece of Matthew's heart muscle with a bioptome.

'Severe rejection,' the cardiologist said to her later as he handed her the results.

Severe rejection. A term that really meant an inflammation of the heart. Alix tried to shake the thought of a heart inflamed out her head. 'He needs another new heart,' she said, diverting to the practicalities.

But then the image of the bioptome's teeth, nipping at Matthew's heart, took over from the previous unwanted picture. She began to think, unscientifically, about what it must feel like to have a biopsy of your heart. Would Matthew love any less because of the void left by each nibbled off piece? And then the segue to Dan's sculpture of the woman biting into her heart. The woman who had lost not just a piece of her heart, but her whole heart, and was alive, regardless. That there might be other people walking around – here in the hospital perhaps, or out at the park, down by the harbour – with a chunk of their heart missing had never occurred to her.

After dealing with Matthew, Alix went to get coffee and watched as a row of male surgeons turned, almost imperceptibly, to present her with their backs, removing from view any part of their faces, anything that could be misconstrued as a welcome.

But she could hear them talking as she stirred her coffee, about the latest divorce. The older her colleagues became, the more they divorced. What wife, what family would put up with, willingly, the hours of a transplant surgeon? Having to leave anything, even the birth of a child, if the call came through that a heart was available. Dan didn't care, he would just work whenever she did and take time off whenever she was home.

'I knew she had the shits with me,' one of the surgeons recounted. 'So I told her to go out shopping for a new outfit then I bought some prawns because she loves prawns and I cooked them on the barbie. I even lit a dozen bloody candles. Had a bottle of French fizz. All set to show her I knew she was pissed off with me for being here all the time when the bloody phone rang. Course that's when someone decides to go ahead and die and give their fucking heart to one of my patients. When I got home later she'd packed her bags. Cleaned the place out.'

None of the other surgeons spoke. Alix wasn't sure if it was because they were uncomfortable from the sharing of too much information or whether each of them could well imagine the same thing happening to them.

Then he spoke again. 'It's bloody lonely without her.'

And Alix did not know what made walk over to him, did not know what made her say this. 'It's your fault,' she said. 'I'm lonely too. But that's *not* my fault.'

The surgeon stared at her and she saw that he was yet another person who'd lost a piece of his heart except the difference was that he'd given his away.

'Fuck off,' he said and she walked away because she did not want to look at another abandoned person, reminding her that there would be no more love for her, reminding her that she was just one more in a team of doctors who were married to a ward full of people whose hearts were slowly dying.

The first contraction came early, at thirty-six weeks into the pregnancy. But it was like a false start because, after that, the baby took a long time to be born. It seemed to not want to come out as much as Alix wanted it to stay inside. 'Can I have an epidural,' was the first thing she asked the midwife when she arrived at the hospital.

'Are you sure? You're only one centimetre. Why don't you see how it feels?'

'I don't want to feel any of it.'

Ten hours passed by somehow, but she was only dilated four centimetres and she couldn't get out of bed because of the epidural, which she'd had topped up every time she even imagined she could feel her toes. She'd read her magazines, eaten her lollies, drunk all the lemonade. And so it went for eight more hours: contractions, a slow dilation, more lollies – one of the midwives had gone downstairs to buy more for her, clearly feeling sorry for this woman whose husband had died – more epidural.

Sleep, they said to her, but how was it possible to sleep with a baby shoving its way out of her and into the world? She did not sleep. Then it was time to push but she was too tired. She did not push once. She could not understand what they were saying to her, to push as if she was having a poo. She was having a baby, not something that she could flush away down the toilet.

Her obstetrician put her legs up in stirrups and he cut her so he could fit the forceps inside and he pulled, hard; she could see his arms straining the one and only time she looked down at what was happening to the other end of her body.

Even then it was not quick; it was still labour, still work, still a relentless quaking and shuddering from just below her breasts right through to the muscles of her thighs, and no, she did not want the mirror, did not want to see where to push, did not want to see exactly what it looked like when an oversized pair of metal pliers had disappeared within oneself to extract something that was perhaps better off left inside.

Then the baby was out. 'It's a girl,' the obstetrician said as he plopped the slimy baby with blue feet and hands on her chest. Alix waited for it to cry but it did not. Instead it stared at her with the blue eyes it had taken from its father and it hardly seemed to blink. It was waiting for Alix to declare her position, perhaps: to renounce the baby or claim her. Alix could do neither because she could not look away from those eyes until eventually the midwife came to take the baby, to weigh it and put a nappy on it and to listen to its heart with a stethoscope.

'Can I?' Alix asked, gesturing at the stethoscope. The midwife nodded and passed the baby to Alix and from then on all that Alix could hear was auscultation, the sounds behind the closed doors of her baby's skin and the look of her father caught and held within her baby's eyes.

CAMILLE

TEN

Paul has rung to say he can't stay with Addie at the hospital today. He has a meeting. With real, live people. So he has to attend. Whereas I am supposed to be at work with people who can be called neither real nor alive. So I have to cancel. I ring my boss and apologise. Because Julie has uni today, Louisa is ill and Paul's mother and sister are at Palm Beach for a long weekend. No one at the hospital complains when I call, how could they? But that is not the point. It's not that I don't want to stay with Addie. It's that I want Paul to not cancel something that you shouldn't cancel. A three year old cannot stay in a hospital room by herself.

When I arrive I look at Addie and forget about Paul. If she remains stable, we can take her home in a couple of days. We can wait there in comfort for her liver until she gets sick again and we come back, thus getting a little bit closer, both to the top of the list and life and a liver, and also to death because to be at the top of the list is to be about to fall over to the other side.

I lie down with her on the bed, not caring about it being daytime and busy and forbidden, because we are leaving soon and I don't need to be nice to anyone any more. I run my hand over her fat little tummy, not round and soft with baby fat but bloated and swollen from the portal hypertension. She looks like a World Vision child with skeletal limbs and a pregnant belly. I pick up her tiny hand, which has never been plump like a little girl's should be; it is like a transparent glove pulled tight over bone and vein. It is bruised and purple from too many cannulas and I kiss each livid spot.

'My sleeping love,' I whisper and am reminded of Pygmalion and his ivory Galatea, clothed and adorned in jewels, kissed every night but always cold and hard and unresponsive. Where is the divide, I wonder, between the clinical and the artistic body, between the brain-dead cadaveric donors I work with every day and my daughter? When does one become the other, when can a mother stop responding to her daughter and see only corpse?

Addie is not cold but she is cool, her skin is not hard but it is bony and she is not unresponsive but merely asleep. I clasp my hands and for the first time I pray to whomever, to Aphrodite or God or some other power, that they bring my work of art back to life.

Addie's life has been an unending experiment, partly because she was our first child.

The Breastfeeding Experiment: a constant guessing game as to whether she was getting enough milk, was the first breast empty and should I move her on to the second breast, and how could such a small mouth accommodate such a large nipple without 'grazing', which is what the midwives in the hospital called the blistering sores that I did not want anybody to touch, let alone suck on. Six weeks later, when the option to breastfeed was taken away by the biliary atresia, I would have done anything to have those blisters back.

There were experiments with formula to improve her poor weight gain. Experiments with vitamins to give her body the things that the biliary atresia took away. Experiments with naso-gastric tubes. Drip feeds of Liquigen and Monogen, a kind of liquid fat, every afternoon and every night. Visits to the hospital almost weekly in winter as a constant snotty nose caused her to knock the tube out. Each time that happened, we would have to drive to Emergency, wait to be triaged, and wait again for a nurse to have the time to reinsert the tube. Three or four hours would pass us by. I bought the girls a portable DVD player because what else can you do with a one-year-old and a two-and-a-half-year-old in a hospital for five or six hours nearly every week?

Sleep, though, was the biggest experiment of all. I remember Addie cried every night from midnight until at least three in the morning for the first six weeks of her life. We rocked the bassinette, patted her bottom, swaddled her, fed her, sang to her, walked with her and, the first night we took her home, I tucked her into bed beside me as she howled, thinking that the feel of her mother beside her, holding her close, loving her, would be enough. It wasn't. I was so shocked at this discovery. That hugging and loving did not stop tears. That being a mother did not stop tears. It was not the magic wand I'd thought it would be.

Paul arrives after work. 'Sorry,' he says as he brushes past and kisses Addie's cheek. 'A defamation suit's been threatened over one of my articles. I had to go through everything with the lawyers. It took forever.'

'Yes,' I reply as I gather my bag. 'I can imagine how slowly time might move in a boardroom full of lawyers as distinct to the brisk pace at which it moves right here.'

'Go home. See Rosie. I've got it.'

'I'll get you something from the cafeteria and then I'll go.'

'I can go down and get something. She's asleep.'

'Guaranteed she'll wake up in the ten minutes you're not here and scream the place down. She's not being sedated any more, don't forget.'

'She'll be fine Camille. She won't wake up and even if she does there are nurses here.'

'I could have been and gone in the time it's taken to have this conversation.'

'Whatever. Buy me a sandwich. Are you going to come back when I need to take a leak? I suppose you don't need the toilet when you're here because you're better than that.'

I turn around, go downstairs and buy him a ham and salad sandwich because I know he hates ham. When I return to the room I pass it to him and say, 'It was all they had left. You can always pick the ham out.'

'Just leave it on the table.' He's sitting in the chair reading the newspaper and I wonder if he waits till I'm gone to touch her or whether men just don't feel that same need, to constantly love their daughters through the touch of their hands and the circle of their arms.

I have only just driven out of the car park when my phone rings. It's Paul, calling, I assume, to be a sarcastic bastard and tell me he has to go to the toilet. I let it ring and then decide to answer just before it goes to message bank. The first sounds I hear are hospital sounds but they are close, too close, too much shouting and the liquid rush of retching.

'She's vomiting blood. She wants you.'

'What did you do?' I screech. 'She was perfectly fine while I was there.'

I hang up, turn the car around, park in the emergency bay and run up the stairs. As each foot hits a step it knocks the same thought into my mind: why am I never there when this happens. If I was three and vomiting blood I'd want my mother.

The amount of blood in the bowl and on the bed and on Addie is filmic, it cannot be real. Blood has spattered on Paul's shirt and face; it is even in his hair. They won't let me near her because they are setting up another transfusion, they are sedating her again and I don't even know if she has seen me come back before she disappears into the planet behind her eyelids, a place where I hope she can always find her mother when she needs her.

'Why has she been taken off the list?' I attack the consultant as soon as he steps into ICU the next morning.

'She's too sick. If we open her up for a transplant now she won't make it off the table.' He has learnt, over the past week, to be direct and clinical with me, not to convert everything into vague kin-speak.

'She won't make it out of this bed without a liver.'

'If she gets through this, she's likely to be one of the most in need.'

I don't hear the *if*; I hear the rest of the sentence because that is the outcome I want.

But the consultant continues. 'She's spiked a fever. It's staph. She needs vanc.'

Staph. Vanc. ICU words, but words I do not need in my job because my patients are never around long enough to contract hospital-borne infections. How did this happen? I've been here for the last twenty-four hours straight; it could not have happened while I was here because nothing bad can happen when I am around.

Mummy's here. Mummy's here. I have been saying this over and over in Addie's ear, it has become like a lullaby as my vowels have become sleepy and less defined, as my voice has shrivelled to a whisper. But *Mummy's here* has not been enough, the protective charm of the words has proved too weak and now all we have to rely on to stop the staph from poisoning her blood is vanc, the drug of Last Resort. Last Resort is a place where I work, it is not a place my child inhabits even though, to look at her, intubated and transfused, you would think she has been there a long time.

So I ask questions, because I can control questions. 'What is her blood pressure? What is ...' until I realise I cannot control the answers and those are the important things, after all.

ELEVEN

The consultant comes back later when Paul has gone to work and I am alone. 'If she recovers and goes back on the list, then you and your husband might want to think about having the work-up done to see if either of you are compatible.'

'We're at that point now are we?' I ask.

'Almost. Not quite. But if we do the work-up now, then when we do get to that point, which is likely to be soon, we'll know if we have another option. It's still a backup plan.'

'Let's do the tests today. I will happily take out part of my liver myself if it makes Addie better.'

The consultant smiles at me. 'I know you would, Camille. But you need to think about the risks to you. Your husband does too.'

'He'll be fine with it,' I reply, thinking, *He'd better be.*

'Camille, we need to talk about it more before we both just rush in and do the tests.' That is Paul's reply when I ring him with the news.

I fire back, 'Or we could do the tests and talk about it later. It's a backup plan; they might not even need to use part of our livers. So let's just do the tests.'

'With you, doing the tests is the same as deciding. If I do the tests today and I'm compatible you'll expect me to give Addie part of my liver without even discussing it.'

'What on earth do we need to discuss? If you're compatible then you'll give Addie part of your liver so that she doesn't die.'

Paul sighs. 'Of course I would Camille. But we need to talk about it. What if you're compatible? They'll take out part of your liver in one hospital. Meanwhile Addie will be in the children's hospital having a transplant. You won't be able to see each other because you'll both be too sick to move. Don't you think she'll want you with her when she's recovering?'

'That's a minor detail. She'll be alive.'

But Paul presses on. 'I'll need to be with Addie because you won't let her be by herself. You'll be in hospital recovering from major, and very risky, surgery. So who's looking after Rosie? We just farm her out to Julie or Louisa for a month or so?'

'You weren't too concerned about how to manage everyone before, not when you knew you could leave it all to me. I've got to go. The doctor's here.' It's a lie and I think Paul knows it but I have better things to do with my time than discuss whether or not it is appropriate for me to want to save my daughter's life.

That night, after I finish having my work-up done, I call Sarah. I need a way to shut out the alarms that sound constantly through ICU, to release the pressure trapped within the walls of this other world, an alien space where nothing exists except me and my child and a bank of machines and a team of doctors and nurses who do all they can even when they have run out of things to do. It is a world without night or day, where you forget what silence sounds like, where you see tiny people swathed in tubes larger than they are.

'How's Addie?' is how she answers the phone, is how everyone answers the phone.

'She needs a liver,' I say because, to me, that says it all, says exactly how precarious her situation is. 'But let's talk about the exhibition instead. I've talked about livers all day.'

'I won't be mad with you if you can't do it any more, Camille.'

And I actually laugh because her words make me realise how despondent I must sound; if Sarah, who never lets anyone get out of anything, is giving me a leave pass, then it must seem as if the world is ending. 'No, I'm still going to do it. It gives me something else to think about when I'm here at the hospital.'

There is a huge sigh of relief from the phone. 'Thank God. Because the notes you've written are perfect. I love the pieces you've chosen. I think we should mount five or six plaques on the wall behind each piece with a quote of a paragraph or so taken from the notes. Then I'm going to publish the notes in full in the exhibition catalogue. If we make the exhibition really spaced out, with plenty of room in between each piece, then people will be able to stop and read the quotes, and maybe refer to the catalogue to read more, while they're there, in front of the piece.'

'Sounds good. I'll send you through some more as I write it.' I haven't sent her anything for a few days because I have reached the point in my mother's diaries where I have been born and I am reluctant to read on now, to see baby-Camille and mother-Alix together, bonding perhaps – or not – in the first weeks of my life. The notes that I've written have been easy to edit so far before passing them to Sarah – take out anything too private – but it hasn't been really personal yet because I have been absent. Now everything will be personal.

Sarah's voice pushes the thought away. 'You haven't got to Jack's paintings yet, have you?'

'No.'

'Do you want me to organise another meeting so he can talk to you about them?'

'Not yet. Let me write it my way first. I know stuff about him from Louisa and from Alix's diaries. I want to see if the story works out without him.' I shake my head even though she can't see me. 'I don't mean without him, literally. I mean without his version of events.'

'You'll have to show him the notes, Camille.'

Next to me, there is the clatter and bustle of a new patient being brought in. I can see a child who is really no more than a baby, about Rosie's age. He is on a ventilator. There is no family with him and I hear the words brain injury, stepfather and Community Services and I know it is not going to end well for that tiny baby and I wonder, how could anyone take the gift of a precious, healthy baby and destroy it, transform it into the damaged and neglected child who lies just a few metres away.

I say goodbye to Sarah and then make another call, even though I know I am not supposed to, but I cannot sit here any longer, detached from the real world, where all there is to worry about is what to get a child for their birthday, not whether they will see another birthday again.

'Camille.' Louisa knows it's me before I even have a chance to speak. 'How are you?'

And I love Louisa for being the one person who asks about me before she asks about Addie. I turn away from the baby next to Addie. I remember Rosie's words from the day before, calling her sister *slow*. I shut my eyes. *Why are there so many dead people? How did I survive? Why is it Addie instead of me?* Questions that Paul would find too pessimistic, questions that Louisa would answer with a big squeezy cuddle, an answer that isn't really an answer.

So I don't ask them. I say, 'I just had a work-up done to see if I can give Addie part of my liver. In case we get to the point where we can't wait for a paediatric donor any more.'

'When do you find out the result?'

'In a couple of days.'

'Is Paul doing the tests too?'

'I don't know.' I pause and then ask, 'What was it like, raising Felicity and me by yourself?'

'Having the two of you was the thing that helped me get through the divorce. And remember that Felicity was five by the time you came to live with us so she could do a lot for herself. It wasn't like having two babies.'

'But I was only two.'

'Which made it easier. Felicity thought you were her baby too. She didn't worry so much about why her Dad had left because she had so much fun looking after you.'

'Did you still love Graham when he left?'

'I did,' Louisa says, then adds, 'Well, I thought I did. Until I realised that he'd stopped trying.'

'Why is love so bloody trying? Shouldn't it be easier?'

I can tell Louisa is smiling and I know I sound like a whingy teenager who thinks everything in the world, even getting out of bed, requires too much effort. But, wise as ever, she says, 'The easy thing is to stop loving someone. The hardest thing is to do is to stay in love. No one ever talks about what a struggle it is, how much effort it takes, not just to stay with somebody and suffer through it, but to stay with someone and still feel curious about them.'

'Curious?' I laugh. 'I would have thought desire and passion were more important than curiosity.'

'If you're curious about someone, even after many years together, then it means you still yearn for them. Yearning comes after passion, if you're lucky.'

Yearning. I remember *The Waltz*, Camille Claudel's sculpture, and realise that I have always imagined the figures in the sculpture as Alix and Dan. But perhaps they are not. Alix and Dan had time enough for passion, but they were dead before they could yearn.

At 2.30 a.m. the little boy next to Addie dies. No one has been to see him except the nurse. At 2.00 a.m., I see his eyes open once, and there is nothing in them; he is already gone and I am glad that he does not know how unloved he is, does not know that, when he most needs his mother, she is not there. Even though I am expecting what happens half an hour later I am shocked when my throat stiffens and I cannot swallow or breathe.

I pick up my phone again, dial Paul, but hang up before I finish. I can't call Louisa again. So I dial another number.

'Fliss.' My sister-cousin, who is now living in Hong Kong with her husband, answers the phone on the first ring, as though she had been waiting for my call. 'She's so sick, Fliss. Addie's so sick.'

'I know,' Felicity says.

Two such simple words. No platitudes. Honesty. At last. It makes me cry. 'They've had staph at the hospital and now Addie's got that on top of everything else.'

'Staph,' repeats Felicity. 'Bugger. You've always been worried about that.'

'She's too sick to have staph. What if the antibiotics don't work?'

'What happens if they don't?'

And there it is. A chance to talk it through. To put everything in my mind into words. To have someone listen. I wipe my eyes and concentrate on my reply. 'She can get sepsis, blood poisoning. Then everything shuts down. Blood pressure drops. Fever skyrockets. No urine output. Her heart and lungs go into overdrive. Then septic shock. The end of everything.'

Please come, Felicity, is the sentence I don't add to what I have just said.

I don't need to. 'I'll book a flight. Richard and I will come as soon as we can.'

'But the baby.' My protest is without vigour.

'I'm only thirty weeks. I can still fly. I'm coming, Camille.'

'Thank you,' I say.

NOTES ON AN
EXHIBITION

THE BROKEN BITS

(Plaster, various sizes. Never previously exhibited.)

How does a child make time pass by so quickly? Alix wondered about this every day as her brain assumed a vegetative state and her body became an armature, a framework to support the physiological necessities of feeding and nappy changing and settling to sleep and pacifying sudden and relentless crying. A framework that shut out any emotion about her situation because how else could she surrender Camille to Louisa's care each day to return to work? But she knew that if she did not do this, then the armature would fail to support anything at all and she would be reduced to residual nervous system activity that made her body appear alive when it was not.

Returning to work was the outward sign that she was not wallowing in it, this muddy grief that wanted to suck her down into a kind of quicksand where she could no longer walk or breathe. So every day she dropped Camille off at Louisa's, went to the hospital, worked, then collected Camille, fed her, bathed her, changed her and put her to bed.

Only after those jobs were done, did she allow herself to wade out once again into what others, she knew, would call self-pity. She would sit in his studio wearing his dusty jeans, holding pieces of plaster. *The broken bits*, he called them, the pieces he had begun but not finished because something was not right about them. The scale of the piece was wrong perhaps, like the one Alix held – a woman whose chest was stunted in comparison to the size of her head. Or it had snapped in two because he'd applied too much pressure with the chisel. Or removing the bodily context had caused the sculpture to look like a piece of nothing, rather than the elbow it was supposed to be.

What would it be like, Alix thought, to be nothing? To be like that elbow. To be like Dan, her mind mocked her and that was when she would pick up the bottle of pills from the desk, pills she had prescribed for herself because she wanted sleep, dreamless sleep, endless sleep, not to wake each morning to the absence that was Dan. She would count them out into her hand. Twenty. That would be enough. Her fist would close around them. She would pick up a glass of water, place a pill on her tongue. Tempting herself. How far would she go?

But then the baby would inevitably cry and Alix would put the pills back in the bottle, close the lid, put it on a shelf up high even though Camille couldn't roll over, much less walk, and go to the baby's room. She would pick up Camille, feed her a bottle, change her nappy, wrap her in muslin and put her back in her cot. Camille would cry. For hours. It was as if she had claimed all of Alix's grief, taken it for herself and was flinging it out into the night-dark room. For the first week or so Alix would do what Louisa had told her; she would pick up Camille and shush her, pat her bottom, rock her, put her in the pram, go for a walk, feed her again, change her again, get a little angry – even though Louisa had told her not to do that – and then she would sit on the floor and cry too, not knowing what to do about anything, not knowing how to make Camille stop when she could not even stop herself.

At about 5.00 a.m., they would both fall asleep, Camille first and then Alix. Usually Alix woke herself up at six o'clock, to get ready for work at seven. But one morning she didn't. She slept right through and was only woken by the sound of Louisa and Felicity opening the door to Camille's room, looking for Alix who should have dropped Camille off at Louisa's house an hour ago.

After that, Louisa would appear at Alix's house at midnight, leaving Felicity at home with Graham, and she would do the rocking and the patting and the walking. At first Alix would try to help too, to take turns, but she would end up in the studio and forget to go back inside.

Because to dwell alone at night with Dan, floundering in memory, was all she wanted.

Alix was back on call by the time Camille was four months old. Because you couldn't be a heart transplant surgeon and not be on call. Nor could you work only during the day.

'It's fine,' Louisa had said to Alix. 'If you get a call at night, just drop Camille off here on your way. And if you're rostered on for night shift, we'll take Camille for the night. It's good for her to be around Felicity. She loves her cousin.'

And Camille did. Whenever Alix picked up Camille from

Louisa's house, Camille would cry, she would want to stay; she would not want to go home with her mother. It would take them an hour or so to become reacquainted, by which time it was bedtime and so the process would begin again the next day. Hugs and cuddles at breakfast. Tears when Alix dropped Camille at Louisa's, tears that would vanish when Felicity came running out of the house to smother her cousin in hugs. Tears that would reappear when Alix returned. Bribery with books and toys and then finally Alix found something that worked.

In despair one night of ever getting Camille to eat anything for dinner in between the sobbing, she took her into Dan's studio and sat her in front of a bucket of water. Alix sprinkled plaster dust into the water; it sat on top at first, floating, making milky patterns. She handed Camille a stirring stick and watched as her daughter solemnly swirled the plaster into the water, the expression on her face the same as Dan's.

From then on, every night, they ate dinner in the studio, playing with plaster in the way other babies played with playdough and Alix would feel as if, for a little while, she had both her daughter and her husband in the room with her, together.

Most days Alix started work half an hour early. She would go straight to the anatomy lab and take out a cadaver, a cold stiff body that had none of the life of her husband's sculptures. Finding a heart and dissecting it, reciting the names of its components – semi-lunar valve, tricuspid valve, left anterior descending artery – and practising her technique so that cutting a heart out of a body became an almost meditative experience, in the way that Dan had always described his work, was what she wanted. She didn't want anyone to ever see even a whisper of hesitation when she faced a patient in the operating theatre.

As she took out her scalpel, it occurred to her that someone once loved this corpse, held its hand, kissed its mouth. She made incisions into the skin and then peeled it away, opening up the chest, finding the smooth bones of the ribs and the blue-grey muscles that sat between. She ran her finger back and forth along the bones as if she were polishing them with sandpaper. Then she took out her bone saw, a harsher, more brutal instrument than anything Dan had used with plaster, and leaned into it so that her weight helped her to apply the necessary force to push the blade through bone.

When that was done she stepped back and looked into the open space she had created, a space that nobody had seen before, a space absolutely unrevealed to those with whom this cadaver used to be intimate. She had to put down the bone saw and move away. Every time she had cut into a body, all that she had seen was something disembodied from the person it once was. Not a secret opening into the unknown, into the now always unknowable, because blood and oxygen no longer animated what she had exposed. Not like Dan's work then; the more he exposed the more there was that became knowable.

Her pager shrieked from her pocket. She picked up the two

flaps of skin from the cadaver's chest and folded them back over his bones as if she was shutting the covers of her diary. Then she ran to the OR.

Blood. It was all she could see. Not an unusual sight in theatre but this quantity of blood was horrific and uncontrolled, like the scene of a murder. Which it was, in a way.

'You've cut right through his heart,' Alix said to the surgeon, saying aloud what nobody else in theatre had, what everyone was too frightened to say.

The surgeon was still holding the saw. Helen was standing by the phone and Alix knew it was Helen who had paged her. No one else would have dared to even think that Alix might be able to save the life of a patient who had been butchered by a male surgeon.

Alix continued. 'It's not the recommended way to open up a chest.'

The surgeon threw the saw aside and swiped at his neck. Blood had hit the ceiling and was now dripping down the back of his gown from above. It was dripping on glasses, on faces, on masks.

'Don't just fucking stand there,' he screamed at Alix. 'Help me get this under control.'

He began to shout directions at the nurses, shooting off one idea, changing his mind, asking for suction and sponges and tossing them aside when they proved no match for the blood thrown out by the patient's severed heart.

Alix said nothing; she kept her face calm, her arms folded across her chest and waited until all eyes in the OR were on her, attracted to her composure, a composure that set her apart from the prima donna antics of her male counterparts.

'There's nothing you can do. He'll bleed out within the next minute.' Alix delivered her verdict, turned and left and could hear in the escalating *fucks*, the exact moment when everyone else understood she was right.

The next day she was called to a meeting. The surgeon who had cut his patient's heart in two had submitted a complaint about her, that she had not stepped in to help when he had asked.

As the two men in front of her went through the complaint, Alix wondered if they could hear how ridiculous they sounded, that they could possibly believe she was somehow to blame for a man bleeding to death all over the OR because another surgeon had not the skill to temper his strength when wielding a sternal saw.

But of course she was reprimanded. The other surgeon was not.

That night, at the hospital, she began the same ritual she had started at home. The ritual with the pills. Tipping them into her hand. Pouring a glass of water. Placing one in her mouth. Rolling it around on her tongue and making a bet with herself that, if her pager didn't go off within one minute, she would swallow first one pill and then another until they were all gone. Luckily – or not, she could never tell – her pager would always beep before a minute had passed. But then, she couldn't remember the last time her pager had ever gone for more than a minute without beeping.

THE CIRCLE OF SOLITUDE

(Plaster, 150 x 52cm. An early work that is unusual in the artist's repertoire for its scale.)

Soon Camille was seven months old and Dan had been dead for over a year. Alix had a whole day and a night off work, such a rare occurrence because then it meant she had to think of something to fill that whole day and a night with, something that would keep the memories of Dan away.

She woke before Camille and lay still in her single bed, which was large enough only for her and contained no empty space. She listened to the sound of nothing, a sound full of the freedom of leaves and weather. Then it was full of nothing but Camille's voice, 'Dadadadadadamabubbadadado.'

They're just sounds, the clinic nurse had said. The *da* sound is easy for babies to say and so they say it first and a lot. It doesn't mean she's calling for her Dada.

Alix rolled over and put on the robe and slippers that he'd bought for her, the robe and slippers that had flowers blooming across them with the effervescence of a Florence Broadhurst print, that he had wanted her to save until such time as she might be at a hospital with a baby, because they were perfect for night-time breastfeeding. Then she walked down the hall, opened the door to her daughter's room and put her hand on the cot.

'Good morning baby girl,' Alix whispered as she leaned over and scooped up a warm bundle, pressing her lips to one sleepy cheek. Camille clapped her palms onto Alix's back and chest and then flopped her head into Alix's shoulder. 'Shall we get your milk?'

Camille curled into Alix's left arm and sucked on a bottle while Alix used her free hand to make porridge, pour juice, stack the dishwasher with last night's dishes, boil the kettle and make rice cereal. Then she and Camille sat at the table and Alix spooned cereal into Camille's mouth and into her own and over the highchair as she told her daughter things like, 'I've got a meeting tomorrow about new forms. I wish somebody would give the department something better to do than redesign perfectly good forms.'

To which the response was 'Mama,' or 'Ah-goo,' or, less frequently, 'Dada.'

Alix agreed to a retrospective of Dan's work in the end. She did it for Dan because she knew he would have liked to have seen so many of his sculptures gathered together, borrowed from buyers and galleries around the country. She did it for herself because she wanted to see his imagination, his mind, retrieved somehow from the grave and brought back to life within the four walls of an exhibition space.

It was the only time Louisa ever questioned her. 'Are you sure?' she asked and Alix nodded, not really listening because she was watching Camille, who was trying to copy Felicity jumping on the trampoline. Camille was three years younger, had only just learned to walk but it seemed to Alix that she was the more skilful.

Louisa repeated herself. 'Are you sure? Alix?'

Alix nodded again but this time she added, 'I never thought much of the phrase "body of work" but now I do. Each sculpture was part of something but I don't know what because I only ever looked at them separately. There was all the time in the world to think about bodies of work, later, I thought. Except now there isn't.'

Louisa looked at her daughter, who was daring Camille to jump as high as the clouds. She opened her mouth to remind them to be careful but then closed it because, Alix supposed, Louisa knew they needed to find out for themselves that reaching the clouds was bound to involve a grazed knee at the very least. Then Louisa turned back to Alix and said, 'Sometimes I feel like his body of work is haunting me. Every time I turn around and see Camille's eyes laughing, there he is.'

'I know.' Alix held onto Louisa's hand and they both watched Camille spin around on the trampoline, her smile shining intermittently in their direction, like a star through windswept clouds.

When Alix left the house to go to the exhibition, her hair had seemed red enough, for once. It was like the colour of the diary she had written in while Dan was in the hospital, a silky, brilliant red, the colour he loved, the colour he told her he wanted to dye plaster so that he could spend every day trying to create an exact replica of her hair, but knowing he could never craft something as beautiful.

She always laughed when he said this. 'Why would you keep trying if you knew you weren't going to succeed?'

'For the joy of making,' he always said and then one day added, 'It must be the same for you. You know the transplants won't always succeed but you do them anyway.'

'But that's for the joy of saving,' she replied.

'Joy or power?' he asked.

She thought about it before saying, 'The joy of power.'

He nodded as though he understood and she thought that in a way he did because he exuded a kind of power through his sculptures. They made people stop and look; they drew people in, made them want to own the beauty. But no one understood that the beauty could be owned by none other than the piece of art.

As she walked from her car to the gallery she felt her feet running just a little, her smile lift in time with her feet, the way it always did when she was going to meet Dan. And she had to stop then, to lean on the balustrade of the bridge because the realisation winded her: she'd thought she *was* going to meet him. Because she remembered thinking, in the hospital by his bed, that he emanated from his hands. Everything in the room that she was about to see also emanated from those hands. So he would be there, in the room, in his sculptures. She had found a way to bring him back.

Except now, looking down into the curdled waters of the harbour, she knew she hadn't.

But she did her best. She looked at every piece. Some she could barely remember. Some had been cast before she knew him. Those ones most interested her because she felt that by looking at them, she had discovered a way to bypass the grave, to find out new things about him, to see into his past.

There was one in particular that made her stop. It called to mind another of Rilke's phrases, about the *circle of solitude in which a work of art exists*. It was a figure of a sleeping man, which was in itself unusual as Dan had preferred to cast sculptures of women. It was not just the fact that the man was sleeping that made her feel as if she had stepped into a private moment; it was the attitude of the head. The way it curved down so that the cheek caressed the shoulder with the lips resting, slightly open, just below the clavicle, as if engaged in an act of sensual discovery of one's own skin.

A male voice jolted her back into the exhibition space, and it was then that she realised the sculptures gained nothing from being collected together because they already contained, within themselves, everything that they had to say about her husband's mind. The sleeping statue held a part of her husband that she never knew: Dan before he was made, the Dan who created the works that made him a Sculptor with a capital 's', the person he'd been before the night she first met him. And so she just stared at the man who had spoken to her, for a time that was much too long.

The man let the silence continue.

Louisa must have sensed her struggle from across the room because she came to Alix's rescue, pointing to the man and saying, 'Alix, this is Jack Darcy. He's a painter. He owns this piece.'

The man spoke. 'I think it owns itself. I'm just lucky enough to have it sitting in my studio.'

Alix knew her face was almost shouting her distrust that this stranger could put her secret thoughts into words. 'What do you mean?'

'Whenever anyone looks at a sculpture, or a painting, they try to recast it to make sense of it, to make it say what they want it to say. But it's never recast. It stays just how it is, how its maker intended it to be. So it owns itself, regardless of what I do with it.'

Alix turned away from Jack and her eyes searched the room, seeing all the pieces she wanted to take back to Dan's now empty studio, each of them like a bead threaded with the beauty of her husband's mind.

The image that most haunted her the next day when she woke on a mattress on the floor of Dan's sculpture-less studio was the memory of the painter's hands pressed to his glass.

Jack's fingernails were not manicured and buffed like the silk of his tie; they were chipped and stained with paint. Artist's fingers, stroking the wine glass just as a brush stroked canvas. Dan's fingernails were always chipped and filled with plaster and he held glasses as if shaping them.

She could barely remember if the painter's eyes were grey or blue, if his hair was light brown or dark, if his skin was tanned or pale. But she could recall the patterns made by the lines on his hands, the size of his fingers and the scar that sat below the second knuckle on his middle right finger.

THE VEINS OF HER WRIST

(Oil on canvas, 20 x 30cm. The first work in the artist's *Shades That Cannot be Replicated* series.)

Alix's phone rang early in the morning. She wondered if it was someone from the gallery calling to talk to her about Dan's exhibition, which she imagined would be judged a success just on sheer strength of numbers in attendance. Perhaps they wanted to extend the run for longer than a month but she wanted the sculptures back, the ones that she was lucky enough to ordinarily have sitting on shelves in his studio. She answered the phone with the word no fixed firmly in her mind.

'Have dinner with me.'

'What?'

'I'd like to take you to dinner tonight.'

The sound of Jack's words from the night before was still caught in her mind like a subject in a painting. She said yes to him because she could not say no to someone who had also been trying to hold onto the same ideas as her.

Dinner was a disaster. Her hair was not at all red, it was limp and flat and most decidedly orange so the only thing she could wear was black. She felt, as she stepped out the door, as though she were in mourning because even the tiny bows at the end of the cap sleeves of her blouse seemed too stiffly tied to be in any way appropriate for something as frivolous as going out to dinner.

Alix had almost lied to Louisa when she had called to ask her to babysit Camille. 'I have to go out,' she had said in her hospital voice as if there was some matter of great clinical urgency, a question of life or death to which she was the only solution. And of course Louisa didn't ask anything further, because Louisa would not do that.

But when Alix dropped Camille at Louisa's and Camille had run straight out to the trampoline, calling, 'Fliss!' in almost unintelligible baby vowels, Alix felt that the least she could offer to someone who had given Camille a good part of her life and her home, was an explanation.

'I'm going out to dinner,' she said.

Louisa finished moulding the last hamburger patty for the girls' dinner. 'With Jack Darcy?'

Alix's voice was reduced to a stutter; she sounded like a child, like Camille; or perhaps she sounded ashamed, embarrassed. She stopped speaking.

'He asked me for your number after you left last night,' Louisa continued, as if it happened every day, men asking her for her dead brother's wife's telephone number.

'Maybe I shouldn't go.' Alix wanted, for almost the first time in her life, someone to tell her what to do, to decide for her, to talk her out or in, she didn't know what.

'Maybe you should.'

Alix tried to read disapproval into the way Louisa put patties in the frypan and flipped them from one side to the other but she could see nothing other than someone cooking her daughter's dinner. So then she tried to clarify what was going on. 'It was just the things he said, about the sculpture.'

'So now you're going to dinner with him to talk about sculpture.'

'Yes.'

Louisa smiled.

The restaurant was new, or Alix thought of it as new anyway; it had opened after Dan died and of course she hadn't been anywhere since then. It was on the harbour and the view should have been spectacular but she couldn't concentrate on the white sailboat that floated by or the broken reflections of light in the water or the lone albatross with the plaster-white wings that seemed to glow as if lit from within. Because how did she talk to a man over dinner at a restaurant when the only man she'd talked to in such a situation for the last few years was her husband? Back then she never had to think about what to say because there was no thinking involved; he was Dan and she was Alix and they spoke about everything.

If it had been Dan sitting opposite her she would have been able to tell him about the way she had viewed the heart that she'd held in her hands today just before she had slid it into her patient's chest cavity. She would explain to Dan that Matthew's body had rejected the first heart and so he was being re-transplanted. That she'd trimmed the heart to fit its new home and was preparing to stitch it in when she felt the heart retract. She'd dismissed the idea and continued to move her hands into the mediastinum when she felt it happen again.

This time the movement was more definite; the heart had recoiled. I am unhinged, she thought. This cannot happen. A heart taken out of a body does not move by itself. It is an illusion caused by the physiological disruption to the body as a result of grief.

She pushed the heart forward and performed that operation with her eyes; she shut off all sense of touch. She saw what needed to be done and her fingers became tools attached to the palms of her hands which performed according to her mental instructions.

She asked the perfusionist to turn the flow down and then calculated; the heart was on ice for four hours. It had to be left in Matthew's body to recover for fifteen minutes for every hour it was on ice. Then she speared the left ventricle with her scalpel. Blood shot out through the opening she had made, taking the pressure off the heart.

Every five minutes of the resting time felt like five hours. But then, as the perfusionist dialled down the heart-lung machine, the heart pumped away. Alix told herself she had imagined the recoiling and asked the perfusionist to begin loading up the heart, to wean Matthew off the heart-lung machine. The heart didn't blow up. Nothing went wrong while she was watching. So she asked for another one hundred millilitres of blood.

Then it was time to close up. She wanted to leave the

theatre and hand him over to one of the residents. But she knew that even putting the wires into the sternum could cause the heart to arrest. So she finished the job.

After six hours of surgery she washed her hands, threw away her scrubs and told Matthew's family that he was still alive. Then she walked down to the park on the south side of the building where no one ever came to sit because it was too cold and dark and where the stone benches were always damp, always waiting for the sun that never came to wring them out.

It seemed that she hadn't grieved properly, hadn't let the grief out and now it was altering her perception of things, so she screamed, into the wind, to dilute the sound. If she screamed long enough and hard enough then she would move on to the next stage, which she believed was called acceptance.

When she returned to the hospital, she was paged within the hour to run to Matthew's bedside. All she could do was watch while the heart that had tried to warn her, died.

Alix started the conversation with Jack with small talk because anything small was manageable, or so she had thought until she'd encountered that rebellious heart. 'Did you enjoy the exhibition?' she asked.

Jack did not respond until the waiter had finished with their drinks order and moved away and then he said, 'Yes. Your husband understood plaster in the way I wish all artists understood their medium. He knew when to let the plaster speak and when to make sure it was impenetrable.'

Alix felt as though she was in an art lecture. Gone were the intuitive comments of the evening before and in their place was something more like a lecture and as impenetrable as the plaster he was speaking about. So she changed the subject. 'I haven't been here before,' she said, gesturing to their surrounds. 'Lovely view.'

'Water views are generally considered to be lovely.'

He thought she was being banal and she was, but a certain degree of banality had to be tolerated in order to get to know someone, didn't it? Or had the rules changed while she'd been married? She remembered that there was little in the way of banalities on her first date with Dan but then why was she comparing the two scenarios unless she thought she was on a date? Suddenly it became very important to understand exactly what his intentions were, as if that would help her to find her way through the evening. 'Is this a date?'

He laughed. 'I'd hoped so. You?'

'I wanted to talk more about what you said last night. I'd just had a sense of something and then you described it. But maybe that conversation was specific to that time and place.'

'Doesn't work in a restaurant with white tablecloths and harbour views?'

'No.'

'So where does that leave us?'

The waiter brought their entrees over, deposited them almost invisibly onto the table, then vanished.

'There's always food,' she said with a slight smile.

They began to eat and were silent while they did, Alix

unwilling to launch into any further banalities and Jack seemingly intent on his meal. It was when she was opening her mouth to put her fork in and of course a piece of lettuce decided to stick on her bottom lip that he looked at her and said, 'Your hair is a shade that a painter could never mix.'

After she had rescued the lettuce and closed her mouth she tried to deflect the comment. 'I thought orange was just a matter of combining yellow and red.'

'It is. But your hair's orange in the same way that a heart is red. In a cliché.'

She put down her fork and stared at him. Why the comparison to hearts? She could almost feel the ghost of the flinching heart dance down the middle of the table. 'Excuse me,' she whispered as she stood, napkin dropping to the floor, and left the restaurant to cross the lawn in front and stand by the water.

He didn't rush straight out to follow her; he left her alone for a good five minutes during which she imagined he'd paid the bill and left. But then he appeared, strolling across the grass as though he'd simply stepped out to take some air. He stood near her but not next to her and pointed to the same albatross she'd seen when she walked into the restaurant. 'Another shade that's hard to replicate. The exact white of the feathers.'

'What do you paint?' she asked as she studied the wings of the albatross, wings that she'd thought before were the same colour as plaster but now she could see they were not so perfectly white.

'People. Bodies mainly. Sometimes heads. Sometimes whole bodies.'

'Like Dan.'

'A bit.'

'Why are artists so interested in bodies?'

'It's not just artists.'

'No.' She smiled. 'I suppose a walk through Kings Cross will tell you that.'

He laughed. 'Not what I meant but you're right.'

'But why take note of the colour of the albatross? You don't paint birds.'

'Because it's the same as the colour of the inside of your wrist.'

The way she reacted was not, she supposed, normal. She didn't smile or blush or try to dismiss the remark, because she heard it as truth rather than flirtation and she wanted, with her surgeon's eyes, to see what he meant. She lifted her wrist closer to her eyes and looked at the skin. She saw that, in one spot, the striations of her veins did stain her pale skin the same colour as the wings of the bird on the water.

She remembers how to kiss a man. She remembers what desire feels like. That is what she thought when she woke the next morning.

They did not return to the restaurant, they did not eat their dinner. They bought an ice-cream from the kiosk and walked home. On the way they did not talk about sculpture or art but they talked about magnolia trees and Iris Murdoch and Moscato.

She laughed. Her hands moved as she talked. She didn't

think about Camille or organs. She turned to him when they reached her front gate and he was already moving towards her as if he knew that she was about to disappear. Before she could, he caught her lips against his, not softly, not gently, not slowly, not even leaving a piece of time for thought. She didn't know how long they stood like that, kissing and kissing and kissing, but it was the first time that she felt unconscious, or thought-less, empty minded of all but sensation.

CAMILLE

TWELVE

What a thing to read and then to write when you are sitting beside your desperately ill daughter and the dead body of an unloved baby is lying in the next bed down. That your mother bought pills with which to kill herself.

I snap my notebook shut and watch as they wheel away a bed that is covered with a sheet; it looks empty but has the slightest mound in the middle, a ripple really, insignificant, reflecting in death what had been the child's plight in life.

In contrast, Alix's gesture was so dramatic, suitable for film or stage but not for the muckiness of life with a baby. I can see her, as she would have watched herself, thriving on the spectacle of what she thought she could do to show everyone just how much she was grieving. I am glad that Louisa has never told me about it, that she refused to give Alix's performance the attention it didn't deserve. False dares and Louisa and wanting to dwell on Dan were the things that pulled Alix back and I pick up Addie's hand and whisper to her, 'Mummy's here,' wishing Alix could see me now, could see what it is to promise to your child that you will always be here.

Suddenly, surprisingly, Paul arrives and after he leans over to kiss Addie's head and before I can say, *I wasn't expecting you today*, he says, 'I'm here to do the work-up. See if I'm compatible.'

Surprise and suppressed tension rush out of my mouth with a whoosh. 'Thank you,' I say and I almost cannot quite believe it when my feet push my body up out of the chair and propel me over to my husband's side so that I can kiss him on the cheek.

His smile is wry. 'So that's what I've got to do for affection.'

I laugh. 'Imagine what I might do if your liver's compatible.'

I can hear him laughing as he leaves to have his tests.

Paul comes back to see me after his tests are complete. 'Why don't you go home and be with Rosie tonight. Give her a bath. Addie won't wake up now she's on vanc and the doctor said it'll be forty-eight hours before it starts to work. I'll come here after work and stay the night.'

'Thanks,' I say and I kiss him again before he leaves for work. Then I ring Rosie and tell her I will be home later to give her a bath and put her to bed.

'Bubbles,' she says to me and I say, 'Yes darling, we can have bubbles in the bath.' She squeals because bubbles are almost as good as kisses at making things better.

I pack up my bag at a quarter to six and watch the minutes tick by until six o'clock. I give him the benefit of the doubt; it is okay to be five or ten minutes late. Then my phone rings and it is Paul.

'I'm with the lawyers. We're in court tomorrow. I'm not going to make it in time.'

I hear the sound of Rosie's joy bursting like the bubbles in her bath but I am too tired to yell so I just say, 'Are you going to be an hour late or four hours late?'

'Probably the latter.'

More answers I cannot control. At that moment I hate my husband. I wish I could pour that feeling into Addie's IV tube because I know it is stronger than staph, stronger than vanc, stronger than anything a human could make or imagine, stronger even than death.

I rummage through my handbag, searching for a tissue. Then my phone beeps. It is Paul, I think, he is coming, it's all okay, we will be fine. But it is Sarah. She has attached a copy of the invitation to the opening night of the exhibition. My name is there, in the centre, next to my father's name. And Jack's.

I send Paul a text to tell him that he'll have to stay with Addie on that night. Because I will be too busy. Being a Curator. Of Art.

In the morning when I stand up I feel in my muscles the cliché: *I got out on the wrong side of bed.* Although bed is now a chair and breakfast is two slices of toast cooked in the Parents' Room, a cubby-hole jammed with tired mothers hovering over a fridge, a kettle and a toaster.

The newcomers are easy to spot. They have notes in pen on their hands, complicated words that describe what is wrong with their children, words they have inscribed on themselves so they can Google them later when the doctors have moved on to the next bed. They flip through the single-serve jams and vegemite looking for butter. Most mornings I open the fridge and extract the hospitality-sized tub of wet, white paste that is labelled margarine and pass it to them.

'Thank you,' they say. They are so grateful until they open the lid and stare at what is inside. I eat dry toast with jam.

Some of the mothers are competitive: *My son's been in for a whole week. He's had two operations and won't be going home for at least five more days.* Until they speak to me. All I need to say is *liver transplant* and they are silent. Or another mother says *coma*. They are silent then too. There is always someone worse off.

This morning I pass on the toast and go straight to coffee. It doesn't help, even though I try copious amounts, wishing it would produce a hallucination – a daytime dream.

I go back to Addie's bedside and the staph is still there and it is too early to tell if the vanc is working. Her blood pressure is stable so there is no sepsis. She hasn't vomited blood for twelve hours. I hold onto small details like these now because the larger picture of taking out her liver and replacing it with another has become too abstract to imagine.

The next day I work a night shift at the hospital, timing it so I can be back at Addie's bedside at the critical forty-eight hour mark. Paul stays with her; the court does not sit through the night so he has no excuse.

I have only been at work a short while, enough to notice a new neuro-consultant noticing me, when I'm told of a brain-dead boy in ICU. He's crashed his motorbike, as eighteen year olds are prone to do. I meet the new neuro by the boy's bed.

'I'm Nick,' he says to me.

'Camille,' I reply.

Nick comes into my office a short time later. I've just finished checking the organ donor registry. Nick is holding two cups of coffee and he hands one to me. 'I noticed you inhaling these earlier. Thought you might need another.'

'Thanks.' I take a sip and then ask, 'Which hospital have you come from?'

'I've just moved down from Brisbane.'

'Stranger in town.'

'Yep.' His mobile rings and he looks at it, says, 'Duty calls,' then leaves.

The consultants have spoken to the boy's family and now it is my turn. The boy is brain-dead: *a corpse generating reusable parts* I once heard a transplant surgeon say. The boy is listed on the organ donor registry but his mother wants more time to make a decision. More information. She didn't know that her son wanted to be an organ donor and she has the final say, regardless of her son's wishes. And it seems she isn't sure whether or not she wants to save someone else's life with a perfectly working, only eighteen-year-old heart.

I sit down next to her and introduce myself. I do not get any further.

'He's still breathing,' the mother, Stephanie, says.

I understand she has not accepted the intensivist's explanation of brain death, or, if she has, she does not think it applies to her son. So I need to start there, before I can even begin talking about the fact that organ donation is a gift of great value. I hope she is not deeply religious or uneducated because both of those factors will make it harder.

I look directly at her, something I know neurologists are not good at doing, and say, 'The ventilator is breathing for him. It's stimulating his heart and keeping the blood flowing around his body. That's why he's warm and pink.'

'He's warm and pink because he's alive.' She turns away from me and looks at her son. 'It's all right honey, I know you're still alive. I won't let them turn anything off. Or take anything from you.'

I know that these words, far from being directed at her son, are directed at me. But I also know that if she's decided not to donate then I need to leave her be; I am not allowed to persuade people to change their minds. I provide information and support, she makes a decision and then we all live with it.

So I say, 'I understood from the doctor that you wanted some more information about organ donation to help you make a decision. Is that right?'

She shrugs. 'Maybe. I don't know.'

'Would you like some more time with your son before I speak to you?'

'No, go on. Say whatever it is you're supposed to say.'

So I speak clearly and calmly, some would say dispassionately, because I have to explain something that is almost impossible to understand with emotion, that can only be understood with logic. 'He will never regain consciousness. His brain has stopped working. The haemorrhage ...'

Stephanie actually begins to scream. To scream like a two year old who has lost a toy. I sit beside her and let her scream, knowing it will exhaust her. She stops after a few minutes and sits and stares at her son's face, holding his hand as if she were the one breathing for him, keeping him alive.

It is always the family who most fear death because they can see it; they begin to know something that had previously been impossible to imagine. The patient is the one without fear and for that I think he is lucky.

I try another approach. 'Your son would have thought this through when he decided to become an organ donor.'

'He's too young to know what he's doing.'

I understand that she wants to recast her son, to change him back into something she can make sense of, not this body in a bed who looks like her son but isn't, not any more. She wants to remake him as her child, as her baby, with a flimsy, dependent body, a body that she owns because it is a body that cannot work without her. But she doesn't own his body. And neither does he, now that he has gone.

'Many people see it as offering a gift. A gift of life to someone else who would otherwise die. Perhaps it could turn this terrible night into one that means something.' I pat Stephanie's hand, the one that is squeezing her son's fist.

'Can it wait till morning?'

I nod. 'It can. There is the potential that your son will become more unstable the longer he stays like this. But you should take all the time you need.'

I leave the room hoping that, by tomorrow, anger will have slipped away under pressure of sadness, fatigue and disbelief. That it will leave behind a desire for renewal, a desire for her son to live on, albeit in a purely mechanical way. That she will see it as the better alternative.

As I walk back to my office, I think about one of those long-ago lovers' conversations I had with Paul on the bed in the studio before we were married. He had asked me why I wanted to move on from nursing and become a donor coordinator.

'It's what I've always wanted to do. Everyone, except Louisa, thought I'd do medicine, like Alix. Because I was smart and had the grades. But I found out about donor coordinators when I was at high school. They didn't exist when Alix was a surgeon. And I thought what a good idea it was to have someone to orchestrate those deaths.'

He shook his head, and I realised I had made myself sound like a god or a devil. I had meant orchestrate as in compose; he'd taken it to mean assist.

I tried to explain myself. 'Everything depends on a certain definition of death and also on making sure everyone understands that definition of death. Most people don't. I mean, what do you think death is?'

'When someone stops breathing or their heart stops. Something like that.'

'That's what everyone thinks. But it's not right. Even if you have a heart attack, the real problem is that there's not enough oxygen to the brain and the brain dies. Death is the irreversible end to all brain and brain stem activity; your heart might beat, a machine can help you breathe but it's not you, not any more, because everything that makes you *you* has died.'

'But don't people come out of comas sometimes? Aren't you scared you'll turn off the machines just before they're about to wake up?'

'No, because people in comas still have brain activity; their brain sends out electrical impulses and we can measure that. But if there's no brain activity, no electrical response to stimulus, then there never will be; it won't come back. That's what I have to try to convince people of because if they don't believe in brain death they'll never donate.'

Paul stood up to make coffee in plastic cups with popstick stirrers. He didn't say anything while he spooned sugar and boiled water but when he gave me my cup and sat back down on the bed, propping my legs over his he said, 'What would you do if I died?'

I shivered. 'You're not going to die but if you did I'd donate your organs. We need lots of young healthy organs like yours.'

'But is it true what you hear about organ donors not being looked after as well as other people when they go to hospital?'

'No way.' I shook my head vigorously. 'Because someone who's brain-dead requires as much care from me to keep their organs going as someone who's not. It's end of life *care*. And I do care.'

'Wouldn't it have been easier to be an artist?'

I hesitated before I replied, almost embarrassed by what I was about to say. But I said it anyway, because it was Paul and I loved him. 'No. Because art is my link to my father. That makes it too fragile to expose to the hurly-burly of a career.'

Things too fragile to expose. What are the notes I am writing for the exhibition then? Yes I have edited and yes I have cut before I pass them on to Sarah but in the notes there is Alix and Dan and things like love and death and birth and grief and, if I am not mistaken, often there is fear. All of these are things too fragile to expose. Alix's love for me – was there any? The episodes with the pills have rekindled a doubt that has always niggled. Alix's love for Dan – too much perhaps. And Alix's love for Jack – not enough to stop the deaths. Underneath it all is the ambiguous feeling I have for Paul, which is surely not love because if that is love, then it is not worth dying for.

I tidy my desk and, as I close the door of my office, my phone rings. It's Paul's number so I send the call to my message bank.

Dread. That is what I feel when he calls me now. Because he will most likely want to cancel something or to break a promise and I dread both what he might do and also what I might say in return. *Fuck off* is something I have never said to him but I can feel those words perched like hawks on the end of my tongue, ready to plummet from my mouth and rip away at the carcass of our marriage.

I stuff my phone back in my handbag, hating it, wanting

to turn it off, imagining what it might be like to not have it by my side all the time, this constant reminder that there might be news about Addie – either good or bad – and I hate that I am so afraid of the sound of my phone ringing. I pass by Stephanie's son's room and I think of him lying there, the one without fear, and I wonder if there will ever be a time when I am not terrified of the past and the present and the future.

THIRTEEN

I head straight to the change rooms, intent on outrunning myself. I step out at the same time as Nick, who is also dressed to run.

'That kind of night?' he says and I nod. 'Where's the best place to run it off?'

I lead the way to my regular route, not concentrating on roads and cars but thinking of the man beside me, the stranger in town, the Anna to my Gurov. I can feel that he runs for himself and himself alone, like me, no iPod, just the sound of thumping Nikes and strained breath for accompaniment. There is no look of fierce concentration on his face, no indication that he is actually running off workday stresses; he looks almost vacant, as if running causes his mind to run too, keeping just ahead, relishing the rush of wind through cells, whilst his body is simply pulled along behind.

We finish my usual circuit more quickly than normal and I am struggling for breath when we stop, having pushed myself to a faster pace to keep up with Nick. 'Thanks,' he says. 'I enjoyed that.'

'Me too.' And I did, even though we did not speak; instead

I imagined what it would be like if he came into my dreams tonight. My next words rush out. 'If you're not doing anything on the twenty-third and you like art, you should come along to this exhibition I'm curating. Lots of people from work are coming and it'll give you a chance to meet some of them.'

'You're an art curator in your spare time?'

'It's a one-off thing.'

'Are you in tomorrow?' he asks.

'Yes.'

'Maybe you can tell me more about it then.'

We are back at the change rooms and are in the way of people coming and going so we separate and go back to our lives.

From one hospital to another. From work to Addie. 'Hi darling,' I say when I step up to Addie's bed. Her eyelids flicker open. Because Paul is the only other person there and I have to share the news with someone I say, 'She opened her eyes.'

Paul jumps up. 'That's the first time.'

'Maybe the infection's gone.'

'Maybe.'

We are standing on opposite sides of the bed, on opposite sides of our daughter, and I feel as though Paul can also hear the words that neither of us want to say: *I hope so.* When did we become hope-less, I wonder, or not hope-less but so scared of the despair that lay at the other side of that four letter word that we can not even bring ourselves to utter it.

'You can go home now,' I say.

'I'll wait to see what the doctor says.'

'Okay.'

And we stand in that spot for an hour or so, both studying Addie, not speaking, but not because we are cross with one another; it is because we know the fear of waiting. I suppose there must be a kind of closeness in not wanting the other to have to endure it alone.

'Fever's gone.' The consultant doesn't bother with formalities. 'She'll stay on the vanc for five days but she's back on the waiting list.'

I bend down to kiss Addie's cheek, brushing my smile along her skin as if that could make her smile again too. As I am leaning over her I feel a hand touch my hair and I look up; it is Paul and he is lifting my hair up and out of my eyes and running his hand over my cheek, just as my lips stroked Addie's.

I smile at him and he smiles too and I really *see* his smile as I have not bothered to see it for some time. It is the same as the first smile he gave me and I wonder if it is not that he has changed or that I have changed but that *we* have changed and, if that is the case, might it not be possible for us to stop being the Paul and Camille we have become and to be the Paul and Camille we always thought we would be.

I even allow myself to hope, for just a moment, that the results of our tests will come back tomorrow. That one of us will be compatible. That we will give Addie a piece of our liver. And that we will all leave here together, ready to go home and be a normal family, not a family as much under attack from the biliary atresia as Addie's liver is.

Addie spends small moments of the night awake and, whenever she wakes, she sees her mother and her father there together, not separately coming and going. She doesn't talk because of the breathing tube, but I tell her that her Auntie Fliss will be here in a couple of days, and Paul and I take turns to sing nursery rhymes to her; he remembers that one of her favourites is 'Sing a Song of Sixpence' and that whoever is doing the singing needs to peck off the nose of everyone in sight, so he leans across and tugs at my nose and then the nose of Addie's nurse. We laugh and I am almost shocked at the sound; it hurts my ears. When did everybody stop laughing? When we came to PICU or before? Certainly, nobody ever laughed in PICU but was that the defining moment?

I cannot recall but find myself saying, 'If we laughed more there'd be more of a reason for her to wake up and get better.'

'There would.' Paul nods then he reaches his hand across and tickles my neck.

The jolt of both his action and the sensation cause me to laugh too loudly, in a kind of half-scream, half-gasp that, before, I would have thought was disrespectful to the other anxious families all around us. But now I stretch my arm over the bed and do the same to Paul. Addie opens her eyes and what she sees is both her parents laughing, together.

Addie is extubated before I go to work and her transfer to a regular ward is planned. She is still sick but a transfer means that there are sicker children around and I am glad to have this point of reference: sick, but not at death's door. I wonder, as I leave, just how many doors death has, because I seem to be surrounded by them, these openings that I never want to hear slammed shut.

At work, my first stop is with Stephanie and her son. There has been no decision on her part; her son will take his organs with him to the grave if she doesn't act quickly and I wonder if she is the kind of woman who also throws out soap dispensers, rather than refill them. I gasp at my own thought. When did I become so hard?

I sit down beside Stephanie and say, 'Tell me about him.'

Stephanie talks for two hours about a boy we all know, who was full of spirit and life, who was just about to start university, who couldn't afford a car and so he'd bought a motorbike even though she'd told him not to, who played cricket in the backyard with his mates every Sunday and who always reminded everyone to wear sunscreen and hats because his father had died of melanoma when he was twelve.

'Melanoma sufferers often need skin grafts,' I say. 'Your son could donate his skin to people who need it, just as his dad needed it.'

Stephanie is silent for many minutes. Then she says, 'I thought you just took people's hearts and lungs, that kind of thing.'

'Patients always need hearts but there are lots of people who need other things to help them live. You can choose what you would like to donate. I can show you the list and maybe you could take a look at it and see if there's anything there you think your son would like to give.'

Stephanie nods and I know that I have won.

I am in my office organising the virology and tissue typing tests when my phone beeps. It is Jack, wanting to meet to talk about the exhibition notes I'd sent him. 'Not now,' I mutter because every extra minute I take increases the risk that Stephanie's son will become too unstable to be a donor and then people who need those organs might die, all because I stopped to send a text message.

I walk back to the patient's room and begin to check his body for any self-administered tattoos or track marks. Stephanie asks me what I am doing every step of the way.

'He never took drugs,' she asserts and I want to tell her about all the mothers who believe just that, only to find out too late that they were wrong. But, in this case, Stephanie seems to be right.

'I need to ask you some questions,' I say to her. 'Some of them might seem intrusive, but we have to check certain things so that we don't unintentionally put anyone in danger. You can have a look at the questions first if you like. You might decide that someone else is the best person to answer some of them.'

'I'm the best person. I'm his mother,' she asserts as if she understands but I know she doesn't, that she won't until I begin.

'Let's talk about your family's medical history.' We start with the easy questions. We have a long conversation about her husband and the melanoma. Then we move on to her son.

'Has he travelled anywhere recently?'

She shakes her head. 'Just the Gold Coast for schoolies week.'

I smile. 'Has your son ever had any form of cancer?'

The answer is no.

'Do you know if he was a smoker?'

No again.

'Could you tell me if he drank alcohol regularly?'

She laughs. 'Of course he drank. He was a boy at uni.'

'Would you say he had more than two standard drinks a day?'

'I'd say he saved up his daily allocation and had it all on the weekend, just like most boys his age.'

'Any history of mental illness?'

'Of course not.'

I look up from the list and smile reassuringly. 'We're almost finished. Not much more to go.'

Stephanie nods.

'Do you know if your son was sexually active?'

'I'm his mother,' Stephanie snorts. 'What d'you reckon? I suppose he was but who knows?'

'I can always ask someone else these questions if you like. One of his friends perhaps?'

'I'm the best person to ask.' She is firm about this.

I continue. 'So would you have any idea how many sexual partners he may have had?'

'No.'

'Was your son heterosexual?'

She nearly chokes. 'Of course he was.'

'You've been very helpful. I'm sorry about how hard this must be. But the information will make sure your son helps as many people as possible.'

She hunches back into her chair. And that is the moment her son chooses to make a movement. Her hunch turns into a complete stiffening of her body and she whispers, 'His arm moved.'

I have been through this so many times before and so many times it has nearly brought everything undone. I stand between Stephanie and her son, trying to get her to focus on me, rather than what she wants to see in the bed. 'The movement was involuntary. It is just residual nervous system activity. It is very common and is not caused by any activity in the brain.'

'Then how did he do it?' She is not demanding any more, not crying, speaking softly, almost forcing the words out of her mouth as if she does not really want to say them or hear them.

'His spinal cord is still active. The movement was like a muscle spasm caused by his spine.'

'Thank you.'

So many families say thank you to me and I don't think they really mean it. It is a reflex of the mouth, involuntary, like the boy's arm moving.

Stephanie looks defeated now, as if she cannot bring herself to follow the circle back to the beginning and start all over again with understanding brain death and what it means. She's given in to tiredness and grief and incomprehension and accepts what would never have been acceptable to her last week: that she would allow her son's heart to be taken out even though he could still move his arm. But this is the beauty in what I do – every day I see people like Stephanie who are heroic enough to give someone who is dying the gift of their loved one's organs. And they do this even though it is so hard to understand what has happened to their own husband, wife, mother or child.

So I finish with the bits that mothers like. 'Some people like to keep a lock of hair, or a handprint. I can help you with that if you like.' The boy's hair is worth saving, I think; it is thick and black and curls loosely against his neck. Mothers and lovers would want to kiss that hair, to feel it melt like chocolate against their lips.

'I don't need hair to remember him by,' Stephanie says.

'I'll leave you with him for a while before we take him to theatre.'

Then, after the boy has been opened and picked and closed, Stephanie comes to find me. 'I'd like to see him again,' she says.

'Certainly. Give me a few moments to arrange it.'

We walk together to see her son. She does not cry, does not say anything. She simply takes a pair of scissors out of her bag and cuts the curls from one side of the boy's head.

NOTES ON AN

EXHIBITION

UNCOVERED TORSO

(Oil on canvas, 150 x 110cm. You will note that the next work shares the same name, although both artists named their pieces independently.)

Jack rang Alix the morning after their first date and said to her, 'Come to my house for dinner.'

'When?'

'Tonight.'

'I'll be there at eight.' It was only when she'd hung up the phone that she realised she'd forgotten about Camille, that it hadn't even entered her mind to consider what she would do with Camille while she went out on a date for the second night in a row. And the next logical thought was: did Jack know she had a child? They knew so little of each other but Alix realised she didn't care, that the not-knowing was somehow more exhilarating than all the knowing she'd done about all the people she knew.

In the end, it was Louisa who came to her rescue, of course. She said to Alix, 'You haven't ever asked me to look after Camille at night for anything other than work. It's not as if you're overdoing it.'

'But it's two nights in a row. And you look after Camille four days a week.'

'She's Dan's daughter.'

And this was why Alix knew that she could ask.

They didn't kiss when she arrived at his house, which was a terrace in Paddington, half done up, half not, a little shabby but artfully so. Inside there was space, so much space, no internal walls, just a white void that did not feel in the least bit hollow because of the abundance of paintings lining the two long walls of the room.

'Can I?' she asked, gesturing at the pictures and he nodded and said, 'I'll get some wine.'

She studied Jack's paintings. A face in shadow. The back of a head. Downcast eyes. A succession of unknowable people.

Then she sat in an armchair and looked some more. Not unknowable, she started to think; it was just that the figures' thoughts were the sort that others preferred not to know. Like the exact shade of grief, which she had believed last night was like the albatross's wings, the colour of veins beneath pale skin, hidden blood coursing through a sometimes translucent exterior.

She hadn't noticed Jack approach until she heard the sound of a pencil caressing paper. She covered her face with her hands and said, 'No.'

He continued to draw and she was torn between getting away from the impress of his pencil and remaining still lest she spoiled his creativity. She peeped through her fingers and said, 'I'm sure I'd prefer a drink.'

He moved closer, stopping for barely a moment to leave a

drink on the table bedside her. 'Aren't you curious to know how others see you?' he asked as he stepped back to his position between her and the kitchen.

She shook her head. 'Is that why people have their portraits painted? I thought it had something to do with vanity and something to do with the instinct for immortality.'

'I paint people to show them the hidden pieces of themselves.'

'Perhaps whatever I've hidden is best left uncovered,' Alix said, standing now.

'I've got it anyway,' he replied, grinning at her.

'What's a painter doing scratching around with a pencil anyway,' she said, crossly.

'I knew you wouldn't sit still long enough for me to do a painting. Let's eat and maybe my cooking will make you like me again.'

'You have five Michelin stars, do you?'

He didn't, of course, but the chicken was tender, the salad fresh and the wine chilled so she relented a little and began to talk. They had another curiously external conversation about things outside themselves but which was engaging and stimulating enough to last them through main course. It was only after he had brought out strawberries and ice-cream that he said to her, 'So what fills your days?'

'I'm a surgeon. I do heart transplants.'

'Another one interested in bodies.'

'Yes,' she said.

'Why?'

'I remember telling Dan it was for the joy of saving. But I think it's also to do with the privilege of going inside, to a person's heart, the repository of so much that's symbolic and imaginary, and seeing what's really there, what it really does.'

'So do you believe in broken hearts and love hearts and following your heart?'

'I believe in love and grief and hope but I don't think they're a function of my heart.'

'So where do they come from?'

'The mind, of course.'

'So everything after Dan died was in your mind and not your body?'

'No.' The instinctive answer came quickly but then she stopped. She could mention Dan in conversation because then she could manage it; he was a person about whom she was speaking, not her dead husband, just a point of reference. But if someone else spoke about him they might not stay within the boundaries of what was safe because even she didn't know where those boundaries were; it was only ever apparent after she'd crossed them. She felt his question was dangerously close to the limits.

'I'll wash up,' she said, standing and taking her plate into the kitchen. He let her go, without politely protesting that he'd do it later; he just sat and watched her walk, then carried the remaining plates to the sink.

There wasn't a great deal to do because he'd already-stacked the dishwasher so it didn't feel awkward for the few minutes to pass in silence.

'I'll make coffee,' he said when she'd finished.

'Thanks. Black with one, please.'

Alix resumed her earlier place in the armchair by the paintings and then, after a few minutes, stood up to see if she could help. But he had disappeared. She waited alone with the music for a short while, decided he couldn't possibly be in the toilet and went to investigate. There was a light on downstairs which she hadn't seen earlier. She felt her way down in the half light cast by the room below.

The stairs led into another large room, which she could tell by the smell and the mess of canvases and brushes and paint was his studio. Her face flushed when she saw what he was doing.

The crude pencil sketch he had made of her earlier was clipped to his easel and she was taking shape on the canvas before him. Her body sitting in a chair, skin naked, face covered by her hands. She was leaning forward so only a rounded shoulder, the curve of a breast beneath her arm, and her calves and feet dropping below the armchair were on view. But it was enough. It was like a confession in all it revealed.

'I don't normally run away from my dinner guests to paint them,' he said. 'But I had to get it down. Didn't want to lose the muse.' He smiled.

Alix knew that running away herself or protesting would not stop what he had already started. He had the sketch and the idea of her, whatever that was; he did not actually need her any more to complete the painting.

She looked around Jack's room, anywhere but at his painting of her and flicked her way through a stack of half-started canvases leaning against one of the walls.

'That's rubbish,' he said. 'Stuff I started and couldn't finish. I've had this half-felt impression of a series of paintings I want to do but the impression isn't making its way out of my hands and into the brush. Might be getting somewhere with it now though.'

'I'm sure your rubbish is probably better than most people's fine art project.' But even she could tell that there was something missing in the canvases, and it wasn't because they were unfinished. They were missing the sense that they mattered, and so they didn't. She said, hesitantly, 'They're lovely to look at but they don't make me want to stop and contemplate them.'

'No, you're right.' He stood up and moved to stand beside her, beside a tall picture window that looked out onto a solid wall of trees. Long white branches pointed up at the stars like fingers stretching to reach constellations, and canopies of green swirled in the wind as though she was lost in a vortex.

Then he began to kiss her lips, much more softly than the night before, his touch was almost imagined, and his tongue like a fine-tipped paintbrush, drawing her into the heart of something that mattered.

UNCOVERED TORSO

(Plaster, 60 x 43cm. It is interesting to note the differences in composition between this work and the previous one, although the subject is the same.)

After they had sex, Alix left Jack's house. He watched her dress and watched her leave but he did not speak. For this, Alix was grateful.

She drove off in her car but she did not go home. She drove past places she had not seen since Dan died, places she had taken circuitous routes to avoid because they were places that made her think of him. Now that was all she wanted.

The French patisserie at Five Ways where they went for breakfast every Sunday if she was not working. It was closed for the night but Alix could still see, through the window, the table they preferred because it was always soaked in morning light and she could taste the coffee that was always brewed strong and bitter.

The antique store on Elizabeth Street where they bought the desk and shelves and chair for his studio. They had gone there one morning after breakfast, intending to browse, to while away an expanse of hours as if there were so many hours to waste. Dan sat down in the chair, leaned back, smiled and said, 'It'd be nice to sit in something like this when I've run out of ideas.'

She'd laughed. 'You never run out of ideas.'

'Sometimes they get stuck though.'

As he spoke Alix could picture him, in his studio, staring at the beginnings of a sculpture, at an armature draped with plaster, seeing not what was there but what he wanted to be there. She could see him stretch his arms up, locking his fingers behind his head. He would arch backwards slightly so it seemed as though his hands were conversing with his brain, finding out exactly what they were supposed to be doing. Then his fingers would move away from his head, taking with them the image he'd had in his mind, ready to transfer it to plaster.

She looked at him sitting in the chair, hands in that familiar posture of fingers consulting with mind. So she went back to the shop after they left and bought him the chair, desk and shelves for his birthday, arranging it in the room one day when he was out so that when he came home the first thing he saw was her sitting in his new chair.

Her next stop was Rushcutters Bay Park, the backdrop for early morning walks or runs, where they rarely spoke, they just moved and felt sunshine and water refresh them, make them ready for the delicate precision of handling hearts and plaster. Perhaps they should have spoken, shared more words, and been less happy with silence.

Alix went to work the next day praying for a transplant. She was in luck. She called in the residents to review the waiting list with her and, even though she had her own opinions, she listened intently to theirs, pointing out where their ideas lacked sufficient detail, praising them for any especially astute observations.

Then it was time to scrub, to remove all trace of the invisible bacteria inhabiting her skin, making sure to get into the webs of her fingers, the folds of her knuckles, the beds of her fingernails. One of the male residents stood beside her, clearly not sufficiently concentrating on his scrubbing because he asked, 'Get up to anything last night?'

'No,' she replied. 'My husband's dead, remember.'

He blushed. 'Sorry, I didn't know.' He turned off the tap with his elbow and before he could turn away she said, 'You're not scrubbed. You've been there half as long as I have.'

And so he turned the tap back on and continued to wash his hands. Alix made sure she took an especially long time so that he had to stay there, in the clumsy silence, until after she had finished.

Once they were in theatre she said, 'Dr Hollander,' to the resident who didn't know how to wash his hands.

'Yes.'

'Let's see you make the incision in the chest.'

'Sure.'

Alix wanted to know if his operative skills were better than his washing skills; it would be a waste of time to train him up and have to transfer him later. She stood right by his shoulder – she'd been taught by her superiors exactly how to make a resident feel as uncomfortable as possible – and watched him cut. Even pressure, clean cut.

'Good,' she said and she thought she saw his hand tremble with pleasure at the compliment and she remembered being that young and eager, remembered what it was like to not be so tired and sad and so she said to him, 'Why don't you cut the sternum too.'

He looked at her and nodded, a small smile of thanks on his face, and she nodded too and returned the smile. She stepped back just a little but showed him where to place the Stryker saw and helped him guide the blade along the bone. All she could hear then was the screeching sound of grated bone.

The retractor went in and the patient's heart was bare before them, pulsing, and Alix felt as she always did at this moment: the thrill of looking inside, of finding the object of so much ambiguity, an object that she knew better than most people, a reddish brown misshapen oval of muscle. Because that was all it was – she was yet to find in these operations any sign of heartache or heartbreak, something heartfelt or heartrending; she was yet to locate the soul.

She took the scalpel and cut open the pericardium so the heart was no longer enclosed in its sac. The patient was handing his heart over to her. And she was about to hand over the role of pumping and oxygenating his blood to a machine.

'Clamp,' she said and it quickly appeared in her hand.

'Dr Hollander, I'll clamp the aorta, you can do the vena cava.'

He stood by her side and watched and then repeated the word, 'Clamp,' and was handed one by the nurses. She saw him assess the heart and then place the clamps in place, thus isolating the heart from the patient's cardiovascular system.

'Good. Scalpel.' She held out her hand and then said to Dr Hollander, 'See the scar tissue there,' she pointed, 'and there, from his previous ops. It's going to be much harder to cut the heart away. You need to feel the scar, where it is thickest and how it moves, and work with it from there.'

She was right, the hardened tissue made the cutting take longer than it should but eventually she was able to remove the lower portion of heart.

'You can cut the aorta,' she said to Dr Hollander. 'Just there, between the clamp and the heart.' He made the cut and she continued. 'Now the pulmonary artery, right near where it emerges from the heart.'

She cut away the rest of the heart, leaving behind the back wall of the left atrium, which would be connected to the donor heart. Then she lifted out the old heart. 'It's enormous,' she said. 'Look at it.'

The big old scarred heart pumped one more time and then stopped. She placed it in a kidney dish.

Then it was time to stop for breath. She had a few minutes before the new heart arrived. Everyone was quiet; it wasn't like a coffee break which was a chance to relax and be social. Instead it was a moment to draw inwards, to focus her mind and energy on what lay ahead: saving the life of the man on the table without a heart.

As soon as the esky was rushed into theatre, she moved to another table, drained iced water out of plastic bags and picked up the new heart. An unscarred heart. She flushed it with cardioplegia to paralyse it and said, 'This one's nice and big too.'

She examined it quickly, found a hole and over-sewed it to stop the blood bursting out when it was filled.

'Okay, we're ready. Stand in close so you can see,' she instructed Dr Hollander as she placed the new heart on the patient's sternum.

It was time for the easy part, the connection, rather than the cutting which was where all the time and effort was expended. She joined the back wall of the patient's left atrium to the left atrium of the donor heart with a suture and then did the same with the right side.

Then she rested the heart. Allowed it to fill with blood slowly. It began to fibrillate.

'Dammit,' said Alix but one shock was enough to establish a regular rhythm.

After that it was time to clean up, to remove the remaining clamps, to disconnect the man from the heart-lung machine, to mop up the chest cavity. 'Suction please, Dr Hollander.'

Then she put the man's chest back together with stainless steel wires. 'Over to you,' she said to Dr Hollander, whose confidence she had felt grow with every successful step he took, just as hers had grown one day in an operating theatre when she had been allowed to play with another man's heart.

She watched him put the patient's chest back together with a line of sutures, so carefully because they both knew that even something as simple as stitching could cause the heart to arrest. But not this time.

'Congratulations, Dr Hollander.' She put out her hand and he shook it.

'Thanks.'

'Come with me to talk to the family then you can monitor the patient. I'll need an update in half an hour.'

And off they went to tell the man's family that they had saved his life.

She went home that night and thought about the operation, about Jack Darcy and about Dan. She remembered the first time Dan had sculpted her; he hadn't taken any drawings or used a photograph or asked her to sit. He'd gotten out of bed in the middle of the night and gone out to the studio to cast her naked torso, just the back, not the front, as well as the back of her neck and her arms holding her hair aloft. Even though it was a view of her back and she was not easily identifiable she knew it was her. He'd created her in such a way that the attitude of her hands in her hair suggested the sculptural ability of her fingers to connect, not just strangers' hearts, but also hearts known to her.

Then she called Jack.

'Sorry I left like that.'

'My ego's taken a bruising.' He laughed and so did she

because, of all the responses she was expecting, that was not one of them.

'We could try again,' she said.

'Which part?'

'Not the running away.'

'Perhaps just dinner then.'

'Just dinner would be great. How's Saturday night?' she asked.

'Good. What about a picnic?'

'You're actually quite romantic.'

'I'm an artist. I've got a reputation to uphold.'

She hesitated and then said, 'What about Rushcutters Bay Park?'

'It's a date. Isn't it?'

'I think we could call it a date.'

A week or so later Jack gave Alix a gift, wrapped by a shop with ribbon and a glossy box. He'd remembered after breakfast that they'd been invited to a party that night and that, although he'd forgotten to tell her about it, he'd bought something for her in preparation.

She didn't mind that he'd forgotten to tell her; he was vague about details and arrangements and things that didn't really matter so there would always be, on some level, things she wouldn't know. But she didn't care.

She took the box and untied the bow and, sitting inside on tissue paper, was a dress, a dress to wear to a black tie party, a long, floor-sweeping dress in dark sapphire blue with an unexpected detail of threaded gold around the hem that would shine in the light as the skirt twirled. It was a dancing dress, a fluid dress, a dress made to move and as she ran the fabric through her hands she looked up at him and said all that she could think to say, which was, 'Thank you.'

But he could always say more. 'If you're not careful I might fall in love with you.'

Somehow, after the party, they became a couple. Her name was written on invitations addressed to him, his name appeared on invitations addressed to her and they assumed they were spending at least Friday and Saturday nights together if she wasn't working. Then he asked if he could meet Camille.

She supposed it was a reasonable question. She did not have a reasonable answer. Why couldn't he meet Camille? Because that would be like him meeting Dan.

When she arrived home that night, she stopped to look in at Camille after Louisa had gone home. She studied her with the eye of a doctor trained to see beneath the skin but she saw what she always did. A red-haired Dan.

Camille stirred and opened her eyes. 'Mummy,' she whispered just before her eyes closed again.

Alix knelt by her bed and kissed her cheek. 'Mummy's here.' And she felt the world reduce to the size of her and Camille and wondered if it was enough.

CAMILLE

FOURTEEN

It should have been enough. It should have been enough. The words pump like a heartbeat in my head as I drive home from work with Alix's diary hidden in the boot, as if that could stop the words from escaping the page. What did she decide, I wonder, not for the first time. Yes, I was enough? Or no, I wasn't?

I look at the clock. I realise I have a small window of time, half an hour perhaps, before Julie is expecting me. So I do something completely self-indulgent. I stop thinking and go shopping.

The opening night of the exhibition is fast approaching and I have nothing to wear. I can't remember the last time I dressed up, had my hair done, painted my nails. I'm not even sure where to go so I text Sarah and she texts back immediately with a couple of suggestions. As luck would have it, the boutiques are just a few minutes away.

I run my hand over rows of dresses, most of them lovely, but none of them right. I have no idea what I want but I know that they will not do. And then I see a dress that is so like the one Paul bought for me many years ago that I stop and take it off the rack. I step into a change room and try it on.

In the mirror I see myself in a sheath of draped black silk-jersey that drops right to the floor. It leaves one shoulder revealed, rather than my back, and I like the sense that it is different to that long-ago dress but still somehow the same. There is a slit at the side of the skirt and I catch a glimpse of my leg which is still toned enough, I think, to wear a dress like this. I watch it being packed into a box at the counter and I can't help but feel excited at the thought of the exhibition and the dress. What Paul might have to say about both.

As I am walking back to my car, my phone rings. I've been expecting a call all day with the results of my work-up. Now, here it is. 'Am I compatible?' I ask.

'Yes,' says the voice on the other end of the phone. 'But ...'

'Yes!' I repeat the word, shriek it aloud, laugh. I wasn't wrong to hope because what I've hoped has come true. I will call Paul. He will laugh too. He won't care any more about the logistics.

'But there's a problem.'

'What?'

'You're tests also showed that you're pregnant. You can't donate your liver.'

'Is Paul compatible,' I whisper, knowing the answer even before it is given.

No.

I hang up the phone. How could I be pregnant? Then I remember the night I cried into Paul's old T-shirt. How was it possible that a child could come out of such lifeless sex?

I do not think about being pregnant as I drive home to collect Rosie. I do not want to spoil anything. Because Rosie is so excited that she is allowed to see her sister. She spends the whole time wanting Addie to get out of bed and play. Addie tries her best at peekaboo and other games, but I can see that she is tiring.

A glance at my watch tells me that Paul will be here soon. I will tell him about the new baby. We will work something out. But I do not know what. How do I abort this baby, kill one child, so that I can help another to live? Which is what I had wanted only a few weeks ago: for a child to die so that Addie might live.

On cue, my phone rings. It is Paul. 'I'm not compatible,' he says and I begin to cry, to tell him that I know, to tell him my news but before I can he says, 'Before I forget, I can't look after Addie on the twenty-third. You booked it into my diary but something's come up.'

The twenty-third is the opening night of the exhibition.

The other two children sharing the room with Addie start to cry, one because her mother is leaving for the night, the other because she doesn't like the cold hospital dinner that has been served to her. I move out of the room and into the hallway. Rosie trails after me, beginning to whinge that she is hungry.

'You have to,' I say. 'That's the exhibition. I sent you a text about it. I booked it in with you.'

'Addie can stay by herself for a few hours. The nurses will be there.'

'She's three. She needs someone she knows with her. And what if something happens.' *Like last time*, I think but don't say.

Rosie starts to wail; a trolley is being wheeled down the hall and the sound is scaring her. I can hear Addie calling from the ward, 'Mummy!'

'I can't, Camille.'

'Then ring around and find someone who can. What about your mum?'

'I tried her already. She said she'd look after Rosie but I can't get anyone for Addie.'

Addie is crying now and Rosie is running away, down the hall, away from the trolley. She falls over and begins to howl.

Everyone is staring at me; I am the mother who cannot control her unruly children. And that is when I say, 'I'm pregnant.'

There is absolute silence on the other end of the phone. So I fill it by saying, 'And I'm a match.'

Paul understands straight away what I am not saying. 'Are you insane?' he explodes. 'You've got one child who's dying so you want to kill our baby to save the first?'

'I've always said that for Addie to get a liver, someone has to die.'

'Not my child.'

'Look, I never said I wanted to abort the baby. I just want to discuss it with you. But you shut everything down. Why is it all so fucking hard?'

'Because it's wrong.'

I have reached Rosie and I pick her up but she kicks and struggles so much that I nearly drop her. 'I'm coming,' I shout to Addie, whose cries have become sobs, gulping, breathless sobs and so I snap at Paul, 'And it's wrong of you to bail out on me on the twenty-third but you don't care about that.'

'It's just an exhibition, Camille.'

'And this is just a marriage, Paul.'

'Is it?'

Fuck you. Again I want to say it but again I don't. Because of the children. But we have no back-up plan: my daughter will have to play the lottery that is the liver transplant waiting list and I have bought a dress that I will not be able to wear to an exhibition that I want to see, no, that I need to see because I have worked so hard on it and I am proud of it and I want you to be proud of me too.

'If you don't look after Addie on the twenty-third then we are getting divorced when this is all over.' I mean the words when they come out and I wonder if I will still mean them tomorrow.

Paul's next words assure me that I will. 'Fine.'

That is it. That is all he has to say after seven years of marriage and two and a bit children. It is not fine. But nor is leaving his sick daughter and expecting that I can be with her every day and every night too. I can't remember the last time I slept. After two night shifts at work in a row on the back of a night shift by Addie's side I can no longer think of anything except the hatred. Strong enough this time to make me never want to see him again.

FIFTEEN

Someone clears their throat behind me and I know that it is Paul's mother, come to get Rosie. Lorraine is standing just outside the door, always polite, never intruding, which also means she never gets quite close enough to anyone.

'You can come in,' I say.

'I didn't want to wake her.' She nods hello at the mothers of the other children in the room.

'She's eating her dinner.'

'But so often she's asleep.' She stands next to Addie's bed, leans down, kisses her cheek and says, 'Are you feeling better?'

Addie nods with a mouthful of ice-cream.

'Well, I'll take Rosie home then,' Lorraine says.

I pass her Rosie's bag and say, 'Just give her some baked beans on toast for dinner. And a cup of milk. She'd like a bubble bath – she'll show you where the bubbles are. It'd be great if she was in bed by seven o'clock.'

Lorraine checks her watch. 'That's not much time. We'd better go then. Come on, Rosie.'

Rosie's tears, only just stoppered up, pour out again. 'Want Mummy. Mummy!' She pulls away from Lorraine and takes a firm hold of my legs.

I prise her arms away, bend down and hug her. 'If you go home with Grandma and are a good girl, you can take this lolly with you and eat it in the car.' I pull a couple of jelly babies out of my bag and hold them up. I know it is bribery, pure and simple, but I have no energy left to be a good mother. And it works of course. Rosie takes the lollies and follows her grandmother out.

'Can I have a lolly too?' Addie asks and I am about to shake my head but I stop and say, 'Why not?'

She chews the lollies slowly, savouring them as if they are something she will never taste again. Then I get her ready for bed, read her a book and she falls asleep before the last page.

Soon, the other two children in Addie's room are asleep too. I tiptoe over to the bathroom and pull the door open quickly so that it doesn't squeak. If one wakes and cries, they'll all be awake within a few minutes. And one of the girls has been left by herself for the night so, if she cries, there'll be no one to soothe her and the other girl had cried from the time her dinner was served until about fifteen minutes ago so I don't think any of us wants to hear any more crying, especially, as now, the girl and her mother are both sleeping the sleep of the exhausted, mouths open, unmoving, snoring.

I have a quick shower, a blast of water on and off in a couple of minutes. I clean my teeth. That is it. No cleansing the face, moisturising the legs, pampering the body. I have time only for the bare minimum required to get through each day.

My recliner chair looks so uninviting with its cold vinyl surface and worn hospital sheets so I sit on the visitors' chair instead and stare at a wall. Then I hear footsteps behind me but I don't turn around because I am not expecting anyone and it is probably a nurse. But a voice, a male voice, says my name. It is Jack.

'I know that your life's all over the place at the moment so I thought it'd be easier if I came to see you,' he says and I remember his text message, the one I haven't replied to. He pulls a chair up next to mine. 'How is she?' He nods at Addie.

'Okay. As well as she can be.'

Jack has a folder on his lap and a photograph falls out of it onto the floor. I reach down and pick it up and realise that it is clipping from a magazine. It shows Jack and Alix at the opening night of one of his exhibitions. They are just walking in the doors together and Alix looks like a publicity-shy celebrity caught in the blast of too many camera flashes. Her arm is moving up to her face and her head is lowered; a plummeting red curl and the line of her cheekbone are almost all that is visible. Her hand is in Jack's but it is not slipped in his palm, it is clenching his fingers.

'More stuff that I found,' he says. 'Tell me if you don't want any of it.'

'Don't you want to keep it?'

'Photos don't help me to remember Alix. Reading your notes did.'

'Thanks,' I whisper and I am touched that I have been able to make him remember a woman I barely know.

'I brought you a copy of the cover for the exhibition catalogue. Sarah said she hadn't had a chance to send it to you yet.'

He hands me a shiny piece of paper that is covered all the way to the edges with a reproduction of a painting. I know the painting, I have already written about it but it looks different now. It is Jack's first painting of my mother. She is seated in a chair, naked and leaning forward, her hand is covering her eyes. Her hand is exhausted, lonely; emotions ordinarily expressed through a face or eyes are clearly shown in her body. Even though I cannot see her face I can see that everything about her has been stripped away, that her skin is a carapace containing almost nothing except a tiny spark that can either be roused or extinguished. I feel for the first time as if I know my mother and I want to step into the painting and sit on the floor by her feet, tucked inside the curtain of her hair. I want her to take her hand away from her face, to have her reach down and touch me.

'Why did it happen?' I ask Jack.

He knows what I mean. He is the only person who can give me the *why*.

'I got cancer.'

I got cancer. Three words that seem to suddenly change everything. 'Cancer,' I say. 'Like Dan.'

'It wasn't like Dan. It was an operable melanoma. I had a bit of chemo and then I was fine. But Alix didn't wait for to me explain any of that. As soon as she heard the word *cancer*, she ran out of the house. The accident happened later that night. On her way home.'

When he speaks I hear the ache of guilt in his voice, an ache I am all too familiar with. I understand why his paintings post-Alix have always been described as raw; it is because he paints his anguish, not just at the loss of her but also at the sense that it was his fault, into every stroke.

I try very hard to remember what Louisa told me about Alix's accident – an accident with a car, is how Louisa described it but wouldn't it more ordinarily be described as a car accident? Was Alix not in a car then? Was she on foot and running, running from Jack and his news, running blindly – or running with both eyes open, straight into the path of an 'accident'?

Then Addie begins to fidget, to writhe almost, in her sleep and Jack apologises for taking my attention away from my daughter and we both lose the opportunity that neither of us seems to want to take, in any case, to talk more about the accident.

'Thank you for coming here,' I say to him as he stands. We kiss one another on the cheek before he leaves.

I turn to Addie and soothe her through something, I am not sure what – a nightmare, pain, it is so hard to tell in a three-year-old – and then I fall asleep, which is a relief because then I don't have to think about anything, especially not the past, which, after what Jack has told me, may have suddenly become the most brutal thing of all.

Louisa turns up at the hospital the next night and orders me home to sleep. 'Spend some time with Paul, love,' she says.

I nod, an automatic movement of the head that means nothing. I watch her organise herself in the chair, moving it so that Addie can see her if she wakes, propping a pillow behind her back so she can rest too. I think about the conversation I had with Jack and wonder again why the accident that killed Alix is the one part of her narrative that has not been turned into story by Louisa. 'Louisa?'

She pulls her magazines out of her bag and places them in her lap. All she needs is a blanket across her knees to become a living picture of comfort. She smiles at me, waiting for me to continue.

I smile back at her, a guardian angel by my daughter's bedside, and say, instead of the question I really want to ask, 'It'll be good to have Fliss here. Only a couple more days.'

'Someone for you to talk to.'

'I talk to you.'

'Not as much as you should.'

What I say next does not logically follow but it comes out anyway. 'I'm pregnant. It means I can't give Addie my liver.'

'Oh, Camille.'

'And I asked Paul for a divorce.'

'Why, love?'

'Because he's never here. He's always at work. He doesn't give a shit about Addie or about me. Who goes to a meeting instead of coming to sit with their dying child? And he just expects me to say, *Okay darling, never mind.* He doesn't care if I sit in here for the rest of my life.'

'Did you say that to him?'

'Yes.' There are tears on my cheeks and I am trying to keep the crying in my eyes and not in my throat or my mouth because then Louisa will hear it. They are angry tears though; I am not sad about Paul but I am mad, so mad.

'Are you sure you said that?'

'I did.' My protests make me sound like a child and I feel like a child, like a two-year-old sitting in Louisa's lap at midnight asking for stories about her mother, loving Louisa but knowing she was not enough.

'What did he say?'

'Nothing.'

'Talk to him tomorrow. When you're not so angry.'

Another subject change. 'Jack Darcy came in to talk to me last night. It got me thinking about Alix's accident. She was driving a car, right?'

'She was in an accident with a car, yes.'

There it is again, that odd wording. 'Whose fault was it? The other driver's? Was Alix tired? Had she been working late?'

'The police made an open finding. No blame was ever attributed to anyone.'

'But that's so ambiguous. Did you try to find out more?'

'No. Because sometimes answers don't help, love.'

I snap off a retort before it can come flying out of my mouth because Louisa does not deserve my wrath which is, in any case, not really directed at her. We both say *I love you* and I leave. But I am left walking through the noisy half-dark of the hospital ward with a thought that is as relentless as Addie's disease. What happens if the version I had depended upon, the version Louisa gave me – *There was an accident, she was taken away* – is nothing but a story? What if Alix left me, which is something entirely different.

I don't go straight home. Instead I ring Sarah and organise to meet her at the gallery. We have paintings to hang, sculptures to place and for a solid couple of hours we direct her staff as to where everything should be positioned. The plaques with my notes are arranged and I have a copy of the catalogue in my hand.

Then Sarah opens a bottle of wine, pours two glasses and we collapse into chairs and chink glasses.

'To you, Camille,' she says. 'It's perfect.'

'So tell me something fun about your life,' I say as I lean back into the chair and sip my wine. 'Let me experience something amusing, even if it's only vicariously.'

'I'm sleeping with Ian,' she says. 'One of the guys who was just here helping us.'

'I thought you gave up sleeping with your employees.'

'He's a contractor so he doesn't count.'

I study her face and then say, 'There's more, I can tell. What else are you up to?'

'I'm sleeping with someone else too. An up-and-coming visual artist who spends more time waiting for inspiration than doing any work.'

'Well, maybe you're distracting him.'

'Oh no, I'm his muse, he says. Supposedly I help him "create". But I can't think of one single thing he's done that seems to be in any way inspired by me. I think he just likes the idea of having a muse. Makes him a real artist.'

I laugh. 'He must love the idea of this exhibition then.'

'He does. In fact I'm sure that's what gave him the idea that he needed a muse. He's not clever enough to think of it himself.'

'You're terrible!' We both giggle as if we are back at uni and boys are the only thing that matters. Then I say, 'What's it like to sleep with two men?'

Sarah thinks for a minute. 'Messy. Sometimes I forget which one I'm with.'

'Do you think they notice?'

'Yes. You always know when the person you're with longs for someone else.'

'I went for a run with a guy from work the other night.'

'Camille! I'm shocked. That's not like you.' Then she loses the fake censoriousness and asks, 'Surgeon?'

'No. Neuro.'

'Cute?'

'Very.'

Then Sarah puts down her glass, shrugs and says, 'Maybe for once you should do something that makes you happy.'

I finish my wine and say, 'But will going for runs with cute neuros make me happy?'

'It probably won't make you unhappy.'

'I would so gladly trade every bit of my own happiness for one fucking liver.'

'Stop thinking of things in absolutes, Camille. Making yourself unhappy will not get you a liver. So, while everything else turns to shit, do what you can to make one part of your life a little bit better.'

When I arrive home, Rosie has already been put to bed by Julie. I lie down on my bed, too tired to go to sleep. I try push everything that I have been thinking, about Alix and Paul and Addie and Nick and Jack, to a space in my mind labelled *Things to deal with later*, a place that seems so full it is likely to spew forth my every procrastination should even one more thing be put off until that long away moment called Later.

When Paul arrives home from work he does not expect me to be at home; I can tell by the clattering in the kitchen as he makes a coffee and brings it up to our room. He turns on the light, sees me on the bed, jumps and spills coffee on the floor.

'Shit Camille, what're you doing here?'

'Lying down.'

He chooses not to respond to the sarcasm so I prop myself up on one elbow and that is when I say to him, 'I meant what I said.'

'You say lots of things, what are you referring to now?' He moves into the dressing room to change into his pyjamas. I wait until he emerges because I do not want to have this conversation through a wall.

'About getting divorced. Once Addie has her liver.'

'I've already spoken to a lawyer.'

No. I stop the word before it escapes.

Paul moves into the bathroom to pee, not bothering to close the door.

It strikes me then that marriage is the most unceremonious of things, providing an excuse to fart and pee and pick the spots on your face in front of another person in a way that you never would in front of anyone else. And these are the things about Paul that I see most of all because we are both usually home together first thing in the morning and last thing at night when the bathroom and thus bodily functions are most in use. It is the other parts of his life that I do not see, just as he does not see the other parts of mine. Surely that means everything is around the wrong way. Wouldn't it be better to see Paul dressed in his suit and conducting an interview where he charms and breaks down his subject, rather than standing in front of the toilet, legs spread, pointing his dick into the bowl and letting out a noisy stream of malodorous urine?

And so perhaps it doesn't matter that he has called my bluff. Because it is hard to imagine missing the things I see most of him, hard to see that divorce should bring sorrow. Not for me. But what about Addie and Rosie? What about the child in my womb who is not to blame for any of this?

'So you have time to talk to lawyers but not to come to the hospital.'

'I didn't want to be accused of holding things up.'

'What about the baby?' I can't help but ask it and I despise myself for the way I sound. So needy, as if I cannot work things out myself.

The toilet flushes. The tap turns on. Then off. The sound of hands wiped on a towel. Paul stands in the doorway.

'If I don't give my liver to Addie because of the baby then what do we do about Addie?'

'We wait.'

'You're not even sorry,' I say.

'I never thought it was a great idea for you to give up part of your liver anyway.'

I shake my head at him. 'I meant about divorcing.'

'Look at you, lying there trying to pick a fight. You don't seem too cut up about it either. You can't blame me for everything.'

'Takes two to tango, right? So it must be as much my fault as yours?'

Paul gets into the bed because it is not in his nature to make dramatic gestures and storm out with a pillow to sleep on the couch. I have to stop a smile at the thought of two people arguing about divorce sleeping comfortably together in the same bed. He rolls onto his side, snaps off the light and says, into the dark, 'Maybe it's no one's fault. Maybe it's just what happens when no one cares enough to stop it from happening.'

It takes all my willpower not to be the one to leave the room with a pillow after that comment. Because, all I can think is that it can't be true. We care enough about Addie and yet we can't stop anything happening to her.

I must fall asleep because I wake myself when I roll over to face the centre of the bed. Paul is facing the same way and I can see his open eyes shine in the dark.

He does not say anything, just reaches across with his

hand, threads it through my hair and pulls me towards him, kissing me, opening my mouth to his with his tongue, and then taking his hand out of my hair and parting my legs beneath my nightie, stroking back and forth with first his fingers and then the palm of his hand. His mouth moves away from mine and kisses the skin of my chest, licking in soft wet circles the skin just outside my nipple until I push my breast closer to him and he takes the whole nipple into his mouth, pulling hard. I begin to come but that is not enough for him; he moves his mouth down my body, catching my clitoris with his lips and I can do nothing but press against him, coming again and again into his mouth, crying out too loudly at the bittersweet, beautiful agony of it all.

I wake up moaning softly, my clitoris throbbing from the remains of my dream. I turn and make sure Paul is asleep and has heard nothing before I slide my hand between my legs and rub myself, trying to replay the dream. But it is not enough and it does not work and I am left with nothing but ache and want and emptiness.

NOTES ON AN EXHIBITION

THE WALTZ
(Oil on canvas, 152 x 111.5cm. The most well-known of the artist's works.)

Alix didn't see Jack for two days because she worked thirty-six hours straight, living on whatever she could get from a vending machine.

When he saw her next he said, 'You're superhuman.'

'I have to be.'

'Not all the time.'

They were at his house because she was too tired to go out and he'd tucked her in bed and brought her dinner on a tray so that she could eat real food and then go straight to sleep.

She took a bite of salad and said, 'I do. I can't cry along with a family when their child dies, I can't faint when I'm covered in someone else's blood, I can't flinch when I examine a hideously obese man. I have to be completely self-possessed otherwise no one gets fixed. My patients want me to be calm because it makes them feel hopeful. They want me to be infallible because otherwise the risks of handing their hearts over to me are too great.'

Jack leaned back against the pillows, arms behind his head, studying her face. 'But sometimes it must bother you.'

'When you begin studying medicine you learn that it's best not to think. If even one of the other students starts to talk about how they feel, then it shatters the illusion that we don't feel. Everything falls apart.'

'It's like a collective art project,' said Jack. 'You all have the sense that you matter because of what you do so you don't want anything or anyone to make you stop believing that.'

Alix laughed. 'I like that. A collective art project.'

Jack didn't laugh. Instead he said, 'Doesn't it just burn you all out in the end?'

And Alix replied, 'More members of the medical profession kill themselves than any other.'

'The exhibition's going to be on February 14.'

They were drinking champagne at a bar because Alix had been awarded a major research grant to lead a team investigating ways to improve the preservation of hearts in transit.

As she and Jack toasted her success, she recalled the look on the faces of her male colleagues when the announcement was made. She would have liked to have thought it was a case of stereotypical male resentment at a female getting ahead but she supposed the look on her face would have been the same if one of them had been awarded the grant instead of her. But that was not something she mentioned to Jack because she was stuck on the date he had just mentioned. February 14.

'I'm busy,' she muttered.

He laughed. 'Yeah, yeah. We'll change the date just for you.'

He thought she was joking. Of course he did, because

what else would she be doing on the opening night of his first exhibition of new work for eighteen months? There was enough time to organise to be rostered off at work, to book a babysitter.

But it wasn't work, it wasn't Camille. It was Dan. Dan would have been dead two years on February 14.

The only benefit that Alix could see in the exhibition was that Jack seemed to have forgotten about meeting Camille because he hadn't mentioned it again. He was too busy painting – what he was painting she didn't know, because he hadn't shown her and she hadn't asked to see. Except for a couple of line drawings of a woman that looked like her but didn't.

'Working drawings,' Jack had said as he laid them in front of her one night.

The pictures in front of her reminded her of Dan's sculpture of the woman with the hole in her chest and the heart in her hand. The woman in Jack's drawings seemed to have something heart-like in her hand also. As Alix looked closer, she could not be sure if the woman was offering her heart or throwing it away. Everything about Alix's own history suggested it could be either. But perhaps the woman in the picture wasn't her after all.

Luckily her pager beeped before she had time to comment and she thanked God for heart transplants as she got into her car and drove away. Jack didn't show her anything that he was working on for the exhibition again.

February 14 appeared on her calendar much more quickly than it should have until she found herself with only half an hour to shower and dress and feed Camille.

'Just three more bites, darling. Look, I'll have one, then you have one, then I'll have one and we'll be finished in no time.'

Camille shook her head. 'No like it.'

'But it's yummy. Sultana chicken. You love sultanas.' Not tonight, apparently. And pretending that Moroccan chicken was called sultana chicken was not working either. 'Okay. Let's put it in the bin.'

Camille grinned. She'd won the nightly dinner battle. Alix ran the bath and jumped in with Camille to save time. She'd have to wear her hair up; there was no time to wash it. But Camille had other ideas. She began to splash. Water sprayed over Alix's hair, drenching one side.

'No!' Alix shouted, grabbing Camille's hand.

As soon as she let go, Camille grinned at her and splashed again.

'I said no.'

Alix held her daughter's wrist tighter this time and Camille wriggled, trying to pull away, hurting her wrist beneath the pressure of Alix's hand. The howling, echoing so loudly in the tiled bathroom, commenced. What Alix wanted to do was this: leave Camille in the bath, get up, take a towel and dry herself. Throw on an old dress and walk out of the house, away, anywhere, to a place where there were no food battles, no splashes, no tantrums, no tears. Where she

IF I SHOULD LOSE YOU

herself was barely there, her body a kind of mist, her mind as insubstantial as breath.

What she actually did was this: she picked up her daughter and turned her around so that Camille's back was pressed against Alix's front. She folded her arms around Camille and held her there, in the bath, water dripping from her hair into Camille's tears, washing them away as if that was enough. Enough to cleanse them both, to scour away Dan and the fact that he was not really dead; no, he was there in the house, in the bath, arms around them both, for a moment as long as the flicker of her pulse, and then he was gone again, rising with the steam of the bath into the ceiling, condensing there, and evaporating.

Jack was early to Alix's house by at least ten minutes, something he explained with a smile more constricted than usual as, 'Opening night nerves.'

He began to walk into the house before Alix could stop him and he saw Camille, in her nightie, sitting on the couch, *Possum Magic* open in her lap.

He walked over to her and held out his hand. 'Hi Camille, I'm Jack.'

Camille backed off into the cushions of the sofa, a reaction she had to all strangers but most particularly men. Jack sat down beside her and pointed to the book. 'Can I finish reading that to you while your mum gets ready?' He'd obviously noticed Alix's shoeless state, the lack of lipstick.

Alix shook her head but there was no need to intervene;

Camille shook her head also, said, 'Mummy,' hopped off the sofa and ran towards Alix.

'I'll put Camille to bed and be down as soon as I can. You can go on ahead if you like; I'll meet you there.'

Jack shook his head. 'They won't start my exhibition without me.'

Alix walked over to the sofa to collect the book. Jack reached out a hand to touch her as she passed and she instinctively pulled away, knocking her shin on the coffee table but not stopping to bend down and rub the bruised skin. She picked up Camille and carried her upstairs, finishing the story about an invisible possum that eats lamingtons and becomes visible, and Alix wondered why life was not truly that simple. As she tucked Camille into bed, kissing her on the cheek and then again just above her ear in the space between her father's eyes and her mother's hair, Alix wondered if perhaps it was but she just didn't see it.

The exhibition was called *Body of Work*. Alix thought what a mundane title it was as they stepped into the gallery, which was an aluminium space of light and air in an old warehouse that had been remodelled into something new.

Jack was whisked away from her by the curator, by his agent, by everyone who stood to make their money out of him that night. Alix wanted to step back through the doors, withdraw before she could see but there were too many people behind her and so all she could do was press forward with the crowd into the gallery which had been set up for this exhibition to resemble a maze.

There were no linear walls hung with paintings in a neat row; instead there were many short walls, each leading around a corner and on to another wall, each hung with a painting.

All of the paintings were of Alix.

And then there was the one in the middle of the labyrinth.

It was a painting of her dancing in the blue dress he'd bought for her a couple of months ago. She looked happy; there was a smile on her face that touched her eyes. What she was smiling at could not be determined because the painting did not show what she was looking at. She was dancing with a man in a suit. Jack had painted the features of her face so precisely that the fact she was not just happy, but elated, could clearly be seen. But the man's face was a blur. It was impossible to tell who he was. On first glance his eyes were coloured like Dan's, the blue of a stormy sky that you could not quite see through, but on second glance the eyes were every colour and no colour all at once. He was no man and yet he was someone she knew because the way they were dancing suggested a kind of intimacy. But then there was the matter of the smile; it was a smile she would only give to someone she loved and she was not giving it to the man she was dancing with.

She stepped closer, then further away. What was Jack suggesting? And if he had set her into the painting, then where was he? The man offstage, brush in hand, receiving her smiles while he concocted an oil-colour version of her.

CAMILLE

SIXTEEN

I am due to start work at seven. Rosie wakes at six so I make her a bottle of milk to drink in her cot while I have my shower. Then I put her into the bed with Paul as I get dressed. He rolls over and kisses her tummy. 'Hello Rosie Posie.'

She giggles and says, 'More,' so he tickles her feet until she is laughing too much to breathe properly. After she has recovered she looks up at me and says, 'Home Mummy.'

'Not today darling, I have to work. But tomorrow we'll go to the hospital and get Addie and bring her home and we can all sit on the couch and watch The Wiggles together.'

'Wiggles!' she shouts.

I bend down to kiss her cheek then look at Paul. 'Julie will be here at eight. There's cereal for breakfast. It's warm outside so just put her in a dress or something.'

'Okay.'

I drive to work quickly; it is too early for the traffic build-up. As I walk down the hall to my office I see Nick coming my way.

'I'm going to get a coffee. Want one?' he asks.

'Love one,' I say and I unlock my office then search in my

handbag for a mirror, making sure my hair is neat and my lipstick on. Then I sit down and wait.

He is back in a few minutes with two mugs of coffee and two apples, one of which he hands to me. 'You look hungry.'

I take the apple from him and bite into it. 'No time for breakfast.'

'Or anything else.'

I run a hand over my stomach. The band of my skirt is loose and I don't know how many kilos I've lost over the last month. Being tall, it doesn't take much to go from looking slim to gaunt. Something a baby will fix within a few months. If I keep it. 'Busy time.'

'I heard about your daughter. How long's the wait going to be?'

He's a doctor and he knows exactly how difficult it is to get a liver. So I know what he's really asking me is how long does Addie actually have, for how long can she afford to wait.

I answer him honestly, tell him what I haven't told Paul because I don't know if Paul wants to hear it or if Paul will even choose to believe it. 'I'd say we need one in the next four weeks.'

'I'll pray for accidents for you.'

'Me too.'

We are both silent and then Nick says, 'A drink might make you feel human for a while. Where's a good place in Sydney to get a drink after work? And you can tell me about your exhibition.'

'There's a bar just down the road.'

'Meet you downstairs at six.'

I nod.

He stands and smiles at me before he leaves. I pick up the files on my desk and begin to work so that I do not think any more about Nick and his smile and the anticipation of what might happen later.

I do not speak to Nick all day. I am not sure if this is a deliberate act of avoidance on both our parts or whether it is just that our business for the day does not cause our paths to cross. I certainly know where he is a lot of the time and I see glimpses of him in hallways, his retreating back, the profile of his face, the sound of his laugh.

I sit in my office, supposedly preparing a presentation for a local school about the importance of organ donation. But instead of assembling snippets of interesting facts designed to appeal to children I am thinking about the man I am going to have a drink with in just a few hours.

Nick is not like Paul; he is not as tall but his physique is more toned. Nick has a runner's legs, with sculpted gastronemicus and carved out quadriceps. His eyes are brown, a light, clear brown and in them I can see what he is thinking about me, that he sees a version of me that I sometimes used to see when Paul looked at me: tumbled red hair, clear and pale skin with just a spattering of freckles across my nose, long legs and a smile that takes over my face when I let it.

I am not smiling now though because I am making myself nervous, worried that the lack of care I have been taking with myself of late will quickly show up when I sit next to Nick in a bar. That he will see the dry skin on my legs, the dull complexion I hide beneath foundation, the jagged toenails that need a cut and polish.

I think, briefly, about what it is like to indulge in desire, to bathe in it, to wrap it around you and your lover like a cocoon. I wonder if I will ever indulge in it again. Then my stomach cramps.

I have been sore on and off all morning. I press my hand against the tiny baby in there. Just a dot right now, invisible but present. Alive.

Another cramp.

'Please don't die too,' I whisper because, with the pains and the possibility of a decision being made for me by a miscarriage, I understand that I want this baby. Having an abortion will not make anything better.

I will the baby to be strong enough to hold on with both hands to the walls of my womb because I know it will not be a smooth ride, that I am too tired and worried. That I am not eating enough. That, even though it might be the easiest thing to do, I will not let this baby go.

Because a mother does not abandon her child.

Then it is time to meet Nick so I take my hair out of its ponytail and let it fall down my back, gloss my lips and wait in my office until I am twenty minutes late, giving him the option to change his mind and leave without embarrassment if he chooses. But he does not.

He smiles when he sees me and slips his hand into mine as soon as we are out the doors and away from people we know. We walk to a wine bar that I know will be quiet at this time of evening, quiet enough so we can hear each other talk but with enough music and people that we still feel we are a part of something.

Nick walks in first and he does not choose two stools by the bar which are on view to all, but a table tucked into a corner where we can look out and watch others but where we will not be noticed by anyone. 'What would you like?' he asks.

'You choose,' I say because I really do not care what we drink; that is not the point of why we are here.

He chooses a Sancerre as if to indicate that he knows what he is doing when it comes to wine, just as he seems to know what he is doing when it comes to everything. He lifts his glass and I lift mine and he toasts, 'To you. You're a stunning woman, Camille.'

'And a married one.' I feel a need to confirm that he knows this now, before it is too late.

'I know.'

'So why not, in a hospital full of single, unmarried nurses, ask one of them to show you where to drink?'

'Because I always want the impossible,' Nick says.

'Which will never make you happy.'

'As you've discovered.'

'As I've discovered.'

I sip my drink and place my glass on the table.

Nick says, 'I thought I'd at least be able to wait till I'd finished one glass of wine before I did this.'

He catches my lips with his and as our mouths and tongues move against one another's I remember that first kiss with Paul by the bar where we shut off the world. It is the same feeling again, as if the place we are in does not exist and we are in a space adrift together, my hand pressed against the hard muscle of his thigh, his hand slipping up my back, thumb stretched out to stroke the side of my breast. And I want to take off my blouse and my skirt, to sprawl in a chair, naked and open to him, just as I would in those fantasies I used to have about men I worked with, back when I loved my husband.

But I draw back and the kiss stops and then my phone rings and it is Addie's hospital. 'I've got to take it,' I say as I slip out of my chair and move outside.

I send Nick a text message as I drive, saying, *Sorry, Addie.* Then I press down hard on the accelerator and speed, as fast as I can, which is not fast enough, to Addie's side.

SEVENTEEN

'She came in an hour ago.' Liz, a nurse who used to work with me but who has since transferred to the children's hospital, has called me with news. What she has to tell me is absolutely forbidden but she does it anyway because she's known Addie since she was a baby.

In ICU, there is a four-year-old girl who drowned in her backyard swimming pool. A machine is breathing for her now and her parents are weeping by her side. This girl has a liver, a perfect liver, a liver that would be sized and shaped to fit Addie exactly.

So I do what I am absolutely forbidden to do. I visit the nurse who coordinates the transplants for the liver team. We have a whispered conversation. I meet Liz in a stairwell.

'There's an urgent listing from Victoria,' I say to Liz. 'That child would get this liver, not Addie.'

'An urgent listing,' Liz repeats.

Another child is Most in Need. More than that; an urgent listing means that the other child is in crisis. And because he or she is in crisis, the liver that is here in the hospital will not stay here in the hospital; it will be flown to Melbourne. The child is probably already on a ventilator with just a day or so left of life. Unless they get a liver.

Liz frowns. 'I had to call you because I thought there might be something you could do, strings you could pull, you know ...'

We are walking back to ICU as we speak. Then I see the donor coordinator who is based at the children's hospital emerge from the drowned child's room.

'Can you find out if the family have consented?' I ask Liz.

She moves off and comes back in a few minutes. 'They want some time to think about it.'

Time. We all need more of that.

Rosie and I go to collect Addie from the hospital first thing in the morning. We take helium balloons and teddies and other useless tokens of joy that we know will make Addie smile. And she does.

'Rosie choose,' says Rosie to her big sister, handing over a balloon shaped like a heart with a picture of Sleeping Beauty emblazoned across it. Addie gives Rosie a cuddle, one pair of thin arms wrapped around one pair of chubby arms and I want so much just to be happy with this moment but, as always, it is the impossible that I want even more.

In between lying on the couch with the two girls wrapped in blankets, eating popcorn and having a Wiggles marathon, I call Liz. There is still no decision.

'If they don't hurry up, the donor will just become un-stable,' I grumble. 'Then there won't be a liver for anyone.'

How heartless I am, I think as I hang up the phone. Here I am calling the child a donor even though she isn't yet and here I am complaining about the fact that the parents need time to absorb the fact that their daughter has died. But I cannot sympathise with them. To do so would be to imagine what I would feel in their place.

Liz telephones back a few minutes later. The family have asked to see the list of organs that can be donated. The donor coordinator thinks this is a positive sign.

There might be a liver for Addie. Except for the child in Melbourne.

I remember an episode of *Grey's Anatomy* where one of the doctors cut her fiancé's LVAD wire; she wanted to make him sick enough to leapfrog another patient who was seventeen seconds ahead of him on the waitlist because a perfect heart was there in the hospital waiting for someone. I thought what a foolish storyline it was, that nobody would do such a thing, take someone they love to the brink of death just in case that could save them. Now I wonder how I can take Addie to that same brink without tipping her over.

An accidental overdose of her medication. An accidental withdrawal of her medication. Both of these things could work. Both of these things could work too well.

I sift flour into a bowl, stir in creamed butter and sugar, measure out quantities of ingredients to make fairy cakes with the same precision with which I administer Addie's medications; double checking the label and the dose against the sheet of paper on which her prescription schedule is noted, always careful to give her the right amount of the right pill at the right time.

The doorbell rings just as I am putting the cakes into the oven. Rosie flies towards the door, calling, 'Auntie Fliss,' as Felicity and her husband Richard come inside for their 'just in case' visit. Nobody says this though.

'Camille.' Felicity's hug is as huge as the hugs we used to give each other as children, snuggled up in her bed together at night whenever I dreamed too much about things I didn't understand. She is wiping her eyes behind my head, trying to mop herself up before the embrace ends.

'How's my niece?' I ask as I pull away and touch her stomach, which is a ball rounded over the body of her growing baby.

'Perfect,' she says.

I don't mean to say it but the words come out unwanted. 'I hope she is.'

Paul comes in then so my terrible thought is lost in a fresh round of greetings. Felicity scoops Addie up off the couch and tucks her onto her lap, helping her to take the wrapping paper off her present.

'Look Mummy,' Addie says, moving her finger towards the Tinkerbell nightie complete with green wings that is nestled in the tissue paper.

'Shall we put it on you now?' I ask and Addie nods as a little smile touches her face.

How I would like to pluck the crescent moon from the night sky and hang it on my daughter's face so she wouldn't need to use up precious energy just to smile. How I would like to see her stand and show us all just how much she looks like a tiny paper fairy in her new nightgown.

'You're beautiful,' I say as I kiss her and pass her a looking glass so she can see too.

A short time later Felicity takes Addie upstairs and tucks her into bed while I serve up dinner. We sit down around the table, Rosie on her Auntie Fliss's lap, Louisa beside me and Paul opposite. I notice Richard stroke the back of his hand over Felicity's tummy when he sits, and they smile at each other.

'Stay in love,' I say suddenly.

Felicity doesn't seem to think my remark is in any way odd, she just nods and says, 'We will.'

This time I manage to stop myself before I say, 'I hope so.'

'What have you been up to?' Richard asks Paul as I pass the plates.

'Legal hassles. The paper's being sued because of something I wrote. It's just a nuisance suit though. Won't get anywhere.'

I stare at Paul; of all the things he has been 'up to', how could *that* be at the top of his mind?

I barely hear Felicity when she asks, 'What about you Camille?' because I am still waiting for Paul to come up with something else, some other thing that has been taking up his time. But he is forking roast lamb into his mouth, chewing, swallowing wine.

So I turn to Felicity and say, 'I went out for a drink last night.'

Before she has a chance to reply Paul puts down his fork and cuts in with, 'How about you guys?' and both Felicity and Richard say, in unison, 'Getting ready for the baby.'

Felicity and Richard are the first to say goodnight. I go upstairs with them to make sure they have everything they need. I linger, talking to them for as long as I can, until I see Richard smothering a yawn. Then I go to my room. But I cannot sleep.

Paul comes up to bed some time after I do, having stayed downstairs to clean up. I pretend to be asleep. He leaves the room an hour later, to watch TV, I presume.

I get out of bed too. My stomach tightens. I gasp. Go to the toilet. There are spots of blood on my underwear. 'Not you too,' I whisper.

I walk down to the spare room where Felicity and Richard are staying the night. My hand rests on the door but I do not knock.

It opens anyway and Felicity smiles and whispers, 'I thought you'd come. He's asleep.' She gestures to her husband tucked into the bed and continues, 'He won't hear us.'

We sit on the couch and as Felicity tucks a blanket over her legs, I am reminded of Louisa. I smile. 'You and your mum are just the same.'

She grins. 'There are worse people to be like.'

'There are.' Me, for instance. Or Paul.

There are so many things to tell her about: the baby bleeding inside me, Addie, Jack Darcy, my mother, Nick, Paul. My mind struggles with where to begin in a way it never has before. At Louisa's house, when Felicity and I lay in bed together, the angst of fights with friends or too many pimples or unrequited love would surge forth and be resolved by morning. But now there is neither angst nor resolution. Just the chaos of destiny whose outcomes require no input from me.

'I met Jack Darcy,' I finally say and Felicity nods. Of course Louisa has told her.

'He told me something about Alix.' I am staring at my wedding ring as I talk; I haven't yet taken it off even though I have asked for a divorce because the ring no longer seems to be a part of my marriage to Paul. It has become a piece of jewellery as easily as his days have become legal hassles.

'If Jack told her he had cancer then maybe that means ...' But I can't say it. I can ask my husband for a divorce, I can kiss another man, I can contemplate giving my child an overdose but I can't say this.

Richard rolls over in bed and mumbles, 'Felicity.'

I jump up. 'You should go back to bed. I'm fine.'

'Stay Camille. I'm not tired,' Felicity says but I am out the door before she can stop me.

I go down to the studio. The light is on and when I open the door I find Paul in there, surrounded by bits of wood, holding a saw, hammer and nails by his side.

'What are you doing?'

'Making something.'

'What? You don't make things.'

Paul doesn't look at me, he stares at the wood in his hands and at pieces of paper that I can now see are drawings, a plan to follow. 'A trike.'

'Who's it for?' The disbelief in my voice is strident and I think if it was me on the receiving end of my voice I would choose not to answer; I would walk away.

But Paul answers with his voice only; I still cannot see his face or his eyes when he speaks because he continues to look at the wood. 'For Addie. I had a wooden trike when I was young. I loved it. I thought she would too.'

The shrill ridicule of my voice. The disdain. The assault. 'What is the point in wasting time making something she might never use? And even if she did, what if it fell apart and she hurt herself? You're not known for being Mr Fix-It.'

I hate myself then and so I leave before he can answer and I stand in the garden wanting to find this hatred that is living somewhere inside me, to cut it out, to open my mouth like a gargoyle and have it spew out because I do not want it, no one wants it, but I do not know where to locate it. All I can do is take it inside with me, up to bed and have it lie there, within me, trapped.

Awake in bed I think that divorce would be one less person to care for, to worry about, to feed and remind and cajole. One less thing to be angry about, the not taking out of the rubbish, the leaving a jar of Vegemite open on the bench long after it is finished with, letting Rosie climb the ladder up to the trampoline even though she is only eighteen months old and when she turns as she reaches the top her elbow slips and she almost falls and cracks her skull on the bricks below.

I realise I have reduced marriage to domestic chores and child-rearing. In none of these instances is there anything about us, about Paul and me. Where did we go? Out with the rubbish, away in the cupboard with the Vegemite, separated by shouting over a trampoline ladder.

There is no husband in all of this, no one to talk to about the liver that could be waiting for Addie if only I could make her sick enough, make her an urgent listing too. Home state would get preference. Then she would be fixed.

There is no one to talk to about how I no longer see death as corporeal, that I do not believe Addie will cease to be just because her body fails her. That I no longer think death means anything, nor do I think that if the parents of the child with the liver were to donate it, it would somehow make sense of their loss, that it would make their loss mean something. It is senseless, it means nothing, just that their daughter is dead and mine is not and how could that be any comfort to them when they do not love my daughter the way they love their own.

What do you think, Paul, what would you say, talk to me please just so I know that someone else is floundering too.

EIGHTEEN

When I wake up I have one tiny moment, not even a second perhaps, where I think, *Hurray*! Because tonight is opening night. My exhibition. But guilt scours the joy away and I am left with a kind of queasiness lodged in my stomach – the omnipresence of the liver we do not have mixing uneasily with a nervous excitement about the evening to come.

At breakfast, where I feed Rosie and Felicity and every-one else but somehow forget to eat, Felicity tells me she wants to do nothing other than stay at home with the girls, so I can do everything I need without having to ring and organise babysitters and be at the mercy of my husband and his lawsuit.

The first thing I do is to visit my obstetrician. The bleeding has stopped. The ultrasound shows that the baby is still there. Alive. Tenacious. I smile. At least one of us is.

Then I go to a beauty salon and have my hair done, my nails done, everything done. The whole time I am there, all I can think is: do I believe in my ability to make Addie sicker, so sick that she will be at the end, a place where I never wanted her to be? I cannot imagine my daughter about to die. But there is another child already brain-dead. And a third child, the one who should get this liver, the urgently listed child, how long till they die too?

But of course I don't have an answer.

When I return home, I have a shower, put on my make-up and get dressed. I step out into the living room and both girls are on the sofa with Felicity, reading a book.

'Oh Mummy,' says Addie.

'Princess!' gushes Rosie and she bounces off the sofa to come over and feel my dress, to lift up the hem and inspect my shoes, to tug on the pearls in my ears.

'Oh Mummy,' Addie says again. 'I want to wear that dress one day when I'm a grown up.'

Oh dear God, what do you say to your child, who may never live to be fully grown, when she asks something like that?

I step over to the sofa, sit down beside her and wrap her in my arms. 'Of course you can. Of course you can,' I repeat as if, by saying it more than once, I can make it come true.

I look over the top of Addie's head at Felicity, whose eyes are running over with tears and I swallow and blink until it is safe to kiss both girls on the cheek and stand. 'Mummy won't be late,' I say. 'Auntie Fliss is going to tuck you into bed.'

Before I leave the house I send a text message to Liz. *No decision yet*, is her response, which I suppose mimics my own lack of certainty about just what I am going to do for Addie.

I'm a little late to arrive, which is a good thing I think as I step through the doors of the gallery, because by the time I get there, the sense that the exhibition is a success is palpable. People's faces are flushed, their voices animated, but they are not just drinking wine and chatting; they are viewing the art and consulting the catalogue.

Sarah waves to me and I join her. I'm introduced as the curator and people congratulate me, ask about Dan, about Jack and about my own work; the pen-and-ink row of deliberately imperfect fragments of bodies. One collector even wants to commission another set of drawings from me. I imagine myself in my father's studio, pen in hand, head bent over paper, drawing imaginary bodies that never die, bodies that I can manipulate – like plaster, like paint – to become whatever pleases me. I say that I am not sure, that I will think about it.

Then it is time for Sarah's speech, for my speech. The applause is vigorous and, while I stand there letting it nourish me, I spot Nick smiling at me. I make my way over to him and he hands me a glass of champagne.

'You're an amazing woman,' he says. 'I hope your husband tells you that.'

I shake my head. 'No. He doesn't. But I don't compliment him either.'

'Because you don't think he's amazing any more?'

'I'm generally not very amazing either.'

The silence that follows is the opening. This is where it begins, an affair, in such moments of bravado, moments where someone loses heart and gives in to the straight-forward simplicity of lust.

But I am always the kind of person to think about the complications. It's my job.

I take Nick's hand and lean over and kiss his cheek. Then I step back and say, 'It would be so easy. But that doesn't mean it's the right thing to do.'

'I hope your daughter gets her liver, Camille.'

'Thanks,' I say, as I slip back off into the crowd.

I wander from painting to sculpture, feeling like the confidante of each piece, that they have shared their secrets with me. Some of their secrets are now told in the catalogues that people hold in their hands and in the quotes surrounding each artwork but I have kept many of the secrets for myself. Because they belong to me; they are a part of me. They are the unseen blood that keeps these works alive.

I stop in front of one of Jack's paintings. It is the biggest in the exhibition and its size is imposing and somehow, on the wall where it has been hung, it looks different to the way I had remembered it.

The Waltz, it is called. My mother dancing with a faceless man.

I move back, to give the picture the distance it requires to notice such details as the visual rhyme between Alix's outstretched hand in the top right of the painting and the edge of her skirt at the bottom. Then a voice, Jack's voice, is beside me and he is quoting four lines of poetry:

Oh plunge me deep in love – put out
My senses leave me deaf and blind,
Swept by the tempest of your love,
A taper in a rushing wind.

'Sara Teasdale,' he says. 'I read that somewhere, later, after Alix died, and now every time I see this painting, that's what comes to mind.'

I am so shocked by the words. By the longing. For two men, for one man, for a dead man, who knows? Did Alix even know? Perhaps what I have thought of as Alix's selfishness is not that at all, but madness.

Oh plunge me deep in love. I can see my mother diving into the deep pool of my father and drowning. *Put out my senses.* So that she would no longer feel. *A taper in a rushing wind.* Not a taper though. A taper does not blow itself out.

But if Alix was selfish in what she did – in what I think she did – at the end, then so am I. I want to take my daughter to her own end, to the edge of the river, a tiptoe before the sand meets the water. Is this what you do for love when you are on the edge of madness?

I go home and lie on the bed, still in my dress. I fall into sleep. Then I am woken by a sound. As I walk into the hall I know that it is Addie. I go into her room and she is lying in bed, weeping so softly; I only know she is crying because of the gasped intake of her breath.

'Darling, what's wrong?' I lie on the bed next to her, pulling her body against mine, wiping cheeks that are so wet I realise she has not just begun to cry, she has been crying for some time. She has been crying while I have been sleeping. 'Why didn't you call out for me?'

'I didn't want to wake Rosie up.'

I remember, as if it is happening right now, all the times we have asked Addie not to laugh and giggle and be too loud when we are putting her to bed, all the times we have told her off for calling out at night for no reason and risked waking the baby, all the times I have put her in her room for time-out, all the yelling I have done at her and I wonder why I wasted so much time on things that matter so little, why I put her in her room for three minutes when I could have spent that time playing tea-parties with her. I think of all the calling out at night I would be happy to have now, if only.

Addie begins to cry loudly now. 'It hurts, Mummy.'

I don't know what it is that hurts, I don't know if it is bodily or emotional, I don't know anything other than I am crying too, so loudly, like Addie. I can no longer tell who is making the sounds that I can hear, a relentless wail, a keening, a lamentation, grief no longer hidden, nor dignified and brave and strong as it is supposed to be but cast out of us and I know with the certainty that I have blood and bones and flesh that my daughter is going to die.

NOTES ON AN

EXHIBITION

LONGEVITY

(Photographs, 10 x 15 cm. Snapshots of the artists, during their time with Alix.)

Alix turned and walked out of Jack's exhibition, calmly, sedately, as if she was just going out for air. She spoke into the silence of the evening and said, 'Why didn't you say that they were all paintings of me?' A question meant for Jack, not for the waters of the harbour.

'What would you have said, Alix, if I had told you?' Jack's imagined voice was quiet and calm; not angry but matter-of-fact.

But he was right, what would she have said? What did she ever say when he asked to meet Camille, when he asked her about the date of the exhibition, when he told her, on the night she wore the blue dress, that he loved her. What could she say? I love a dead man as if he were still alive.

She went home and found Dan's mask and then went into Camille's room and lay down on the bed beside her, holding on to the only solid things she had left of him.

And then she saw something. A groove on the mask that she had not noticed before. It sat just below Dan's ear and was only slight, barely an indentation, certainly not a furrow like the wrinkles beneath his eyes, but it was there nonetheless and she did not know what it was.

This mask had touched Dan's skin, it was fixed to the truth of him; it contained nothing that had not been there when he died. Yet there was this mark that she could not recall. Had it always been there or had she damaged the mask in some way? And was it worse that she had forgotten something that was always there or to lose him all over again by damaging the mask, the only thing about him that was still real?

The next night she called Louisa and lied. She said she had to stay at work a little longer and asked her to look after Camille until she had finished. Of course Louisa agreed. Then she paged Dr Hollander.

'Do you have plans this evening?' she asked when he arrived.

'No, no plans. What've we got?'

He was expecting her to say something like, *Fifty-two-year-old male with congestive heart failure,* but instead she said, 'Dinner. Bistro Claude.' It was the same restaurant that Jack had taken her to on their first date and she felt the need to go there again, with someone else, to have a different date to the one she had had with Jack.

'Sure.' His eagerness was endearing. 'My shift finishes at seven.'

There was no albatross sitting on the harbour that evening. There was just water, black like a shadow of the sky, stretching towards cliffs decorated with small stars of light. The waiter showed them to a table by the water and they sat down and ordered drinks.

'I don't think I actually know your first name,' Alix said after she had sipped her wine.

'It's Greg.'

'Alix.'

'I know.'

They were silent and Alix looked at the man across the table, Greg, and wondered what she wanted from him. Not conversation. He would want to talk about transplants and try to praise her work or impress her with how much more he knew than the other residents. And she couldn't imagine having sex with him; he was too young. What would it be like to have those lusting eyes fixed on her naked body, his hands stroking her limbs, his lips burrowing in to the most intimate parts of her? But if she didn't want dinner, conversation or sex then what was she going to do with him?

She finished her wine. He was handsome. Had screwed half the nurses at the hospital or so she'd heard. Maybe that was what she wanted. A quick fuck in the car with someone who had to answer to her the next day at work.

'Alix.' It was not Greg's voice. It was Jack's.

She should have remembered, or perhaps she had; he was going to dinner that night with a curator from Melbourne who wanted to run the *Body of Work* exhibition. She hadn't asked which restaurant he was going to but she should have known. This was his place.

'Jack. This is Greg,' she said.

Jack did not say hello, did not offer his hand. Greg began to offer his and then withdrew it when it became apparent that it was not wanted.

Alix continued. 'Greg and I work together.'

'Not too many people needing transplants around here.' Jack's voice was lighthearted but his eyes were fierce; he was accusing her of something she hadn't even done, didn't even know if she wanted to do.

'No, there aren't,' she agreed.

'Why did you leave last night?'

An understanding of at least part of the situation he had found himself in was beginning to show on Greg's face but he had not the strength of character to say anything or to extricate himself. He just sat there, unspeaking, listening.

'I was tired.'

'You found out something about yourself last night.'

'You're very arrogant, to assume your art can be so trans-formative.'

'Where did you feel it when you fell in love with me?'

Alix was so thrown by the question, out of context as it was, that she did not make the obvious protest, *I'm not in love with you.* Instead she said, 'Nowhere specific. Body parts don't have feelings.'

'If I stub my toe it hurts. What if I stubbed your heart?'

'You're making the assumption that if you did something to hurt me I'd feel it in my heart.'

'No. Just that you'd feel it.'

Jack turned and walked back to his table. Alix folded her

napkin, stood and said to Dr Hollander, 'I think we can safely say that we won't be having dinner tonight.'

She walked out to the front of the restaurant, to the grass by the harbour, where she had gone that first night with Jack. She closed her eyes and when she opened them the albatross was there, sitting on a broken stump, drying his wings. The feathers on the underside of his wing were just visible in the moonlight and she turned her arm over to look at her wrist, at the veins colouring her skin. Then she held out her arm to Dan, to take, to kiss, to change the colour with the stroke of his lips but he didn't so the grief stayed where it was, not lodged in her heart but there in the veins of her wrist, pumping steadily around her body.

Alix wrote a letter to Jack. It was a goodbye, a parting explanation and she felt it was a good and thorough explanation until she reached the last line. *I love you as much as I can and I keep his face because he will need it when he comes back.*

Two things shocked her about that line. The first was that she had written the words *I love you*. Those words had come from her mind down to her hand, into her pen and onto the paper. She hadn't planned to write them. *I love you. I love you.* She loved Dan. She loved Camille. *I love you.* She loved Jack.

The second thing that shocked her was the last part of the sentence. *He will need it when he comes back.* When was Dan coming back? It had been two years and he had not come back.

She took out the mask and she remembered when she and Dan had become lost in the lanes of Florence, when they had visited the gallery with the death masks. Her arrogance, declaring that Dan was not to die and that, even if he did, she would be able to fix him. To bring him back. But of course she could not.

She had thought that having Dan's face in her hands was like holding his soul because his face was the most faithful representation of him that she could have. But it was nothing like his soul. The plaster was cool and hard and surely his soul was more than that. She stood and folded the letter to Jack, put it away in her desk then found a box and packed Dan's face away.

It was midnight when she knocked at his door. Camille was sound asleep on her shoulder and Alix wondered if late-night outings such as this would have some kind of lasting negative effect on her when she grew up. But then Jack opened the door and Alix was only aware of the lasting negative effect of not making this visit.

He was wearing a pair of pinstriped pyjama pants and Alix wished she was asleep against his chest just as Camille was against hers. He said nothing and turned around, leaving the door open, which Alix took to be an invitation in the absence of any conversation. She placed Camille on the sofa, covered her with a blanket and looked at Jack.

He was standing between her and the front door. He was

neither in the room nor out of it and Alix didn't know how to begin to have a conversation with someone who was there but not.

'I'm sorry,' she said and did not say for what, in particular, but added, 'I'm sorry for everything except having met you.'

'And that's the one thing I'm sorry for,' he said and she wondered what the point was in continuing but as Camille rolled to her side Alix was reminded too clearly that the only thing she now had left to lose was her daughter and that would not be an outcome of this conversation, whatever happened. So she continued.

'I was going to say that I wished I hadn't done what I did but I'm glad I did. If I hadn't, we'd have broken up anyway because I would have found another way to make us stop. Stopping was the easy thing to do. I thought I was still going on with life, being strong, that I hadn't stopped because I looked after Camille and went to work. But it wasn't me doing those things. It was what I had left of myself. It was just a layer of skin over bones, organs functioning, heart still beating, but hollow. And that's what I wanted to be like. So how dare you try to fill my heart with feelings? But now I think: how dare I refuse to be filled.'

He shook his head and she thought that was it; she had lost him. But he walked towards her and shrouded her in his arms. She laid her head on his chest and listened and knew she did not need her stethoscope to interpret the sounds that she heard, the auscultation, because she understood it at last.

The months that followed were romantic, sentimental, passionate; a fabrication, a falsehood. Because romance belonged to imagination, to art, to a week in a life. Not to the sustained longevity of the everyday. Not for Alix anyway.

They were always together, Alix and Jack and Camille, burying their feet in the sand at Bondi, putting a star on the top of a Christmas tree, jumping on the trampoline at Louisa's while she made them dinner. The kinds of things you might see in a painting, lovely to behold until you realised that the people caught there would have only those moments because they were stuck forever in oil on canvas.

CAMILLE

NINETEEN

Addie is now considered to be in a critical condition, much to Paul's pleasure. To him, this means things are happening at last. He does not understand how waiting lists work, that Addie isn't first in line, that another child is at the top of the mountain and Addie is still to face the climb.

She is now awaiting resurrection, a kiss from a storybook prince or a bolt of electricity passing through God's hand, miracles, which of course I don't believe in. I believe in the drowned child in PICU with a liver to donate.

This child is just a few beds down from Addie and I think, if only my hands could scoop that liver out of her and stuff it inside Addie before anyone noticed then that would solve everything.

I walk down to her bed and pretend to be stretching my legs as I look. She is only a little bigger than Addie. Her hair is blonde and she looks like the type of child people would notice, would stop to tell her mother how beautiful she is and her mother would be so gratified, more so than if she herself were told she was beautiful; she would reach out a hand to her daughter, to brush the hair out of her eyes and say, 'Thank you.' I know because that is what I do.

As I watch the girl I see her through her mother's eyes, in a way I have never seen a donor before. Her cheeks are blushed with life, her chest rises and falls, her skin is warm and soft. I remember my high-school Shakespeare, the unveiling of Hermione's effigy in *A Winter's Tale* and the lines Paulina utters: *prepare/To see the life as lively mock'd as ever.* And Leontes' reply, *Would not you deem it breathed? and that those veins/Did verily bear blood?*

Brain death. What a mockery it is, what a mockery of life. How can anyone believe in it? How can anyone believe that that the living person before them is really dead?

I walk back to Addie's bed and everything seems to be around the wrong way. She is the live one yet she does not look it. The girl down the hall is pinker and more peaceful and it is easy to imagine that she is simply asleep. Addie is as thin as my finger bones, her skin so white it appears that her veins no longer bear blood and in sedation she is not reposeful; she is annihilated, everything has been knocked out of her, including, it seems, life.

Not five minutes have passed before I walk back to the other girl's bed. The curtains have been pulled right back and I do not know how long I stand there but I suddenly realise that the father and mother are staring at me as if I am appalling. And I am. Because I am coveting their dead daughter.

I turn and run. Run hard. Run fast. Run away from the

person I have become. Leave that person standing beside a hospital bed. That person who thought she could fly up close to the gods and play games with another child's life. Play games with her daughter's life.

I get in the car and drive to Jack Darcy's house. It is still the same terrace in Paddington that my mother visited so many years ago. It's distinctly grand now, renovated, classic, all shabbiness polished away.

I knock on the door and hope to God that he doesn't have a wife at home to answer the door.

'Come in,' he says when he sees me, as if it were an ordinary event, the daughter of his long dead lover appearing on his doorstep without warning.

I blurt everything out as we walk down the hall, before we even sit down because I feel as if I don't say it then I may lose my courage. 'I'm the same as her. As Alix. I saw it in the painting last night.'

Jack shakes his head. 'You're like the Corinthian maid.'

'What?'

'The Corinthian maid who traced the shadow of her departing lover on the wall so she had an image to remember him by.'

I shake my head; I do not understand the riddle, how it relates to girls with livers and girls without, what it has to do with me and with my mother.

'The shadow body of her lover is a thing outside him. My painting of Alix isn't Alix; it's something outside her too.'

'You're telling me not to read anything into it.'

'The painting will only tell you what you already know. I don't know you well, Camille, but it doesn't strike me that you've ever thought you were like Alix.'

And then I say it. 'She killed herself, didn't she?'

Jack sighs. 'She wasn't driving a car. She was on foot. There was a footpath beside the road. But she wasn't on it. '

'Of course she wasn't!' I'm shouting now, not at Jack, at myself. 'Why did everyone love – no, fucking adore – someone so selfish?'

'Did you finish reading her diary?'

'What?'

'After she left my house she went to Dan's studio. Louisa only found out later that Alix'd been home because of the diary she'd left open on the desk. It had the date. And the time.'

'I didn't read the last few pages. I had enough stuff for the catalogue and then Addie got sicker and ...'

'And you didn't want to know. Nor did I, for a long time. But if you read it then you won't waste time wondering about it, inventing what she might have said, making it into the worst possible thing. You'll just know, and then you can live with it.'

I speed back to the hospital. On the way, my phone beeps. A text. Addie. Something's happened.

I don't even pull over, I just yank the phone out of my bag and open the message. But it's not about Addie. It's another secret that I shouldn't know.

The urgent listing's been removed. But I didn't tell you that.

'Oh,' I whisper. There are only two reasons why the urgent

listing would have been removed. The child received a new liver. Or the child died waiting.

The liver is Addie's.

I press down harder on the accelerator. Drive onto the wrong side of the road to overtake cars. Just two minutes from the hospital, the road is being repaired. The cars are trapped, going nowhere.

I pull over onto the footpath. Pedestrians shout at me, 'What the fuck?'

As I rush into ICU, the drowned girl's body is being wheeled away.

I run forward, towards her bed, and her family stare at me again with slapped-face shock. I spin around and scream at Felicity, 'What happened?'

'It's not Addie.'

'I know it's not Addie. But she's taking Addie with her.' I am so loud, everyone has come out to see the woman standing in the centre of intensive care, reaching out to a trolley carrying a dead girl who is not her own.

Then Liz whispers in my ear, 'They're not going to donate.'

I shout at the girl's mother, 'Why not?' but she does not look at me; she looks down at the cloth covering the body of her daughter, that is all she has eyes for, that is all she sees.

Felicity pulls me away and wraps her arms around me, saying my name, 'Camille,' over and over just as Paul walks in and hears my howl, which is a sound that every parent in ICU turns away from, because it is a sound that they all want to make as they watch their children die.

TWENTY

Hours pass. Addie's monitors shriek. Her body starts to fail. By the end of the day she is an urgent listing. I have got what I wanted without having to do anything.

As I sit beside Addie's bed I read Alix's diary. These are her last words.

> Jack was so matter-of-fact about it, like Dan was; and his words were almost the same. I've got cancer. I did not need to hear any more, the prognosis, the number of months, the treatment plan because none of those things are about the real thing which is death. I cannot fix death; I tried, but Dan never came back.
>
> And yet, in the space of that one word, cancer, Dan has come back.
>
> Tell me Dan: if you are your body and your body is gone then aren't you gone too? You don't feel gone. I thought you had but here you are. My open eyes cannot see you but when I shut them, there you are behind my closed lids.
>
> You are in the studio, looking up and smiling when I open the door. You are wearing your work jeans, the ones with rips and holes and plaster crusts, the ones

that you shake the dust out of, watching it fall through the air, tiny refracting motes.

You are here in that sculpture and in that one. They were all sculptures of me but now they are not. They are about you. When I look at them, I can see the way you carved my eye socket as you gave that sculpture the ability to look out and into the eyes of its viewer. As you let that sculpture tease the viewer into thinking it was a woman's face they beheld, when in fact it was you they were seeing all along. You are everywhere and yet you are nowhere.

But what if you were somewhere and I could go to that somewhere too? Did you put that thought into my head or did I? Perhaps you are one of Rilke's terrifying angels because now you tempt me into thinking that there is a way – a way to see nothing but you.

I drop the red and gold book, drop my mother's words, her selfish, stupid, stubborn words, into a bin.

As I stand, staring down at the diary nestled amongst latex gloves and syringe wrappers I remember other words that described my mother. Her obituary, a piece of newspaper that I kept throughout childhood and into adulthood. The words on that piece of paper said that my mother was a renowned surgeon, the first female heart transplant surgeon in NSW, a trailblazer. That she saved the lives of many terminally ill patients in her short but illustrious career.

But how many lives didn't she save? I wonder. How many did she squander? At least one.

There was always, before, a possibility, even a likelihood, that it had been an accident. But there was also something unsaid and this unsaid thing has lived in my body since I was two years old, not growing, not festering, just present, like a heart, an essential part of me; without it, I would not be who I am.

She stepped off the kerb and into the path of the car because she wanted to. She didn't stumble or trip or forget to look both ways before she crossed the road. It was not an accident. There was Jack. There was his cancer. And there was my mother with one dead husband, one dying lover – or so she thought – and a knowledge better than most of how to die.

As it hit her, did she think? Or was there only the skin beginning to break, to bruise, to split open, her skeleton cracking into pieces, no longer a body but a series of broken white bones, just like Dan's sculptures. A tibia on the road, a femur on the path and a scapula stuck in the front grille of the car, a heart pushed into her back, ripped from its berth, smashing against the cliffs of her ribcage, battered with lost blood.

I remember what Jack had said to me, just half an hour ago. *You'll just know, and then you can live with it.* And he's right.

I pull the diary out of the bin, read over the last, the very last, of my mother's words. I think how funny it is that, until now, I had believed Rilke's words – every angel is ter-rifying – because all the many unknown things about Alix had frightened me so. Now as I sit by Addie's bed all I can see is the waste – that Alix could be so careless as to never consider what it might be like at some moment in the future to hold her granddaughter's hand.

TWENTY-ONE

Everyone knows that a three-year-old is too young to die. But only the good die young. What kind of person would invent such a truism? Not a mother.

Was Addie good? Sometimes yes. Sometimes no. Every time we went for a walk she would pick flowers from the neighbours' yards and when we returned home, she would hand them to me and say, 'I love you Mummy.' She always held her sister's hand, without needing to be asked, when we crossed a road or walked through a car park.

But take, for instance, a time when she was eighteen months old. Rosie had just been born and I was trying to resettle her, to get her to sleep. Addie stood in the middle of her sister's room, screaming.

Her mouth was stretched open so the skin on her lips looked as though it might split. It reminded me of one of my father's sculptures, the one he used to call the lady trap because he and my mother had met in discussion over it. Alix had thought the mouth in the sculpture was saying something that no one wanted to hear. But Addie couldn't speak well enough to say all the things she wanted to say, the things that no one wanted to hear such as, *I hate my new sister, I want my mummy back, I hate that Mummy picks Rosie up more than me, I want my sister to go away, I hate, I want, I hate, I want ...* So she was using the only sound she knew that declared what she felt.

And now Addie is frozen like that, mouth open in a mute wail, like the figure in Edvard Munch's painting.

I want to freeze myself in the same way, to tip back my head and unseal my mouth. To undo my voice and cast my scream out, out beyond me and into the ears of everyone, so it reaches up to the roof, inflates the sky, and fills my daughter's empty body with its reverberation, its echo, and that the power of this scream would be enough to bring her back from the silent screamless place to which I have lost her.

Felicity finds me sitting beside Addie's bed, making records of a death that has not yet occurred, but which I can feel close by, in the room. I show her what I have been writing and say, 'If I don't do it now, I'm worried that I won't be able to when the time comes.'

But she doesn't tell me off or accuse me of being morbid. She says, 'When we were growing up, even though you were younger, I always wanted to be like you.'

I laugh. 'Bet you don't now. See, I can still joke. I'm coping.'

Felicity smiles at me. 'And that's why I wanted to be like you. Because you coped with everything. There was nothing you couldn't handle. Even when you were little you were completely self-assured. One day, when I was grumpy because it was raining, you said to me that all I needed to do was ask you to fix it because you knew how to talk to the clouds and you could tell them to go away. I believed you and you went outside, stood in the rain and shouted at the sky and within a minute, the sun started to shine and a rainbow appeared. You had the biggest smile on your face when you came back in and I thought you were supernatural.'

I shake my head. 'I don't remember that.'

Felicity touches my hand. 'You don't always have to be the one who makes the rainbows appear. Let Paul try sometimes.'

I am about to say, *I do let him but he won't*. I don't say it though because I know that somewhere along the way I decided that I was the only one who could make the rainbows shine for my children. So then he stopped trying to make them shine for anyone, including himself.

TWENTY-TWO

I leave the hospital for half an hour to go home and get supplies. A change of clothes. Clean underwear. A real coffee. But instead of gathering those things together, I walk into my father's studio and stare at the moon.

I am thinking of the new baby inside me, just as my father thought about his wished-for baby. The baby he named Camille, back when I was just a dream. *My very dearest down on both knees before your beautiful body which I embrace.* Rodin's words to that other Camille. Words between lovers; they could also be words from a mother to her child.

I put Alix's diary away in the drawer of Dan's desk but, as I do, a folded corner of paper juts out. I am about to push the paper back into the book until I notice that it has been tucked away beneath the back cover. I pull it out and read it. It is a poem. Rilke. His 'Slumber Song'. Copied out in Alix's hand.

Then I see a movement outside, on the driveway. It is Paul. He is pushing something and then he sits down on it. It is the tricycle he was making for Addie, finished now, with smooth, varnished wood, a silver bell and a rainbow of streamers flickering from the handlebars.

He folds his legs up so his knees almost touch his chin and he puts his feet on the pedals. He bends his arms, holds the handlebars and begins to cycle so the bike moves, awkwardly, hesitating; his legs are too long to relax into any kind of smooth rhythm.

I watch him ride, up and down, clownish really, ungraceful, but that is not what I see. I see love that I have overlooked, love that I have forgotten. Love for our daughter that he has kept too well disguised out of a fear of losing her. We have lost so much and there is so little left, which is why I go downstairs, step outside and watch him.

He cycles up to me and stops. 'It's finished.'

'It is.'

The moon is adrift in cloud now; I cannot see Paul's face and he cannot see mine. So I say to him, 'The girl who died in PICU, the one I was crying about; I wanted her liver. I wanted to do something to Addie that would make her nearly die so she would get the liver, so another child who was sicker than Addie wouldn't. I didn't care about that other child. And I was going to do something to Addie.'

It is so dark outside it is as though my eyes are shut and I am looking at not just the inside of my lids, but the inside of myself.

Paul's reply is seemingly unlinked to anything I have just said but when I listen to him I hear that it is his inside space. 'I made you stay in the room with Addie because I couldn't. I cried the whole time I was there, except when someone else was in the room and then I tried to make them angry so they would go. If I went to work then I didn't feel as though I was nothing but a coward.'

Of course it would have been so much better to have said these things to each other before. But perhaps we wouldn't have heard them the way we are hearing them now. Not just the words, but what sits underneath, the blood flowing below the skins of our sentences.

He continues. 'It'll be nice to have another baby. I want to have another baby, Camille. And I want to be here for the baby.'

I step towards him. My head tucks into his shoulder and one of his hands intertwines itself in my hair, the way it has always done since we first met. So much has passed between us since then. Since we fell in love at a party long ago.

As I think of that Paul and that Camille, I remember how fearless we were. Unafraid to speak to one another. Unafraid to be in love. Unafraid of loss, because we did not know what loss was. I don't know when the fear began. Of becoming estranged. Of losing Addie. Of never being worthy of art in the same way Alix was – adored, captured, transformed. She was like the Lady of Shalott, seeing the world after my father died through the mirror of grief and then dying at last when she looked upon reality – that death could not be undone by her; she was not heroic, but ordinary. You lose so much when you desire the romance over the real.

I look down, over Paul's shoulder, at the trike he has made for Addie and I know that I no longer want to be the one without fear. The one caught in plaster. The one smashed to pieces on the front grille of a stranger's car. I know that in losing Addie I might do what my mother did because it would be the only way to stop missing my daughter.

But I will not. Because there is Rosie. And the baby inside me. That is what will stop me. My children.

'I want to show you this,' I say to Paul and I put the poem from Alix's diary into his hands.

'*Some day,*' he reads, slowly, aloud, '*if I should ever lose you/will you be able then to go to sleep/without me softly whispering above you ...*'

Death is not a single act of the body. If I should ever lose Addie's body, I will still whisper things to her, every day: *Look at the butterfly; Sleep tight my darling; Mummy's here.*

I hear Paul's voice drift away with the final lines of the poem – a precious love left alone in a garden full of star-anise. He pauses then says, 'When I was making the trike, I pictured her riding it through the park across beds of flowers.'

I laugh. 'That's the kind of thing Addie would do.'

A simple thing. But real. And very lovely.

Here is Paul, here is Rosie, here is Addie. Here am I. We are around a hospital bed certainly. We are waiting, together.

ACKNOWLEDGEMENTS

As always, the biggest thank you goes to my husband and children. This book wouldn't be here without you.

Thank you to the staff and patients at St Vincent's Hospital, Sydney, for meeting with me and answering my questions, of which there were many. Special thanks to Dr Emily Granger, Transplant Surgeon and a truly inspiring woman. Thanks also to staff at Donate Life NSW and at the Victor Chang Cardiac Research Institute, in particular to Anna Dear and Alasdair Watson.

An early draft of this manuscript was completed during a residency at Varuna, The Writers' House, and I thank them for much needed writing time and space. I also acknowledge the support of the Australian Government through the Australia Council, its arts funding and advisory body, in providing a grant for this book.

Many books provided me with valuable information and ideas for this novel. These include Elizabeth Presa's essay, 'White Work', for introducing me to Rilke and to Rodin's works in plaster; Christine Montross's memoir *Body of Work: Meditations on Mortality from the Human Anatomy Lab*, for explaining so eloquently what cutting into a corpse is like; Kathy Magliato's memoir *Healing Hearts: A Memoir of a Female Heart Surgeon* for detailing the barriers a female faces in her profession; Marina Warner's *Phantasmagoria* for the idea of the death mask; Lesley Sharp's *Strange Harvest: Organ Transplants, Denatured Bodies, and the Transformed Self* for alerting me to the role of the donor coordinator; Rainer Maria Rilke's *Selected Letters 1902–1926*, his *Duino Elegies* and his poem 'Slumber Song', which also inspired the title for this book; and Joan Didion's wonderful memoir, *The Year of Magical Thinking*, for its insight into the effects of grief. I have also quoted from Sara Teasdale's poem 'I am Not Yours'.

Nicola O'Shea's editorial advice was invaluable and it inspired many new ideas. Finally, thanks to Fremantle Press and Georgia Richter, especially for the title idea. It's been wonderful working with you again.